He would not abide a man who bit another man. That was child's play, not proper fighting. His fist connected hard with the man's cheek and nose, made a crunching, snapping sound as it hit. Slocum felt the nose smear sideways under his knuckle, and it felt good, considering the nonsense these jackals had doled out, and all without knowing him.

The man continued to snap his stumpy teeth, squirm, and now gurgle on his own blood, but he didn't stop his thrashing attack. He was frenzied, so Slocum gave him another hard drive to the face. This one landed above the man's cheekbone. Slocum had had enough experience in the manly art of pugilism to know that his punch had delivered the ingredients of a black eye to the rascal. He'd wake up tomorrow with a throbbing blue, purple, and yellow shiner.

That blow slowed the man's writhing to a random but weakened struggle. Soon, and with a little more help from Slocum's tightening arm, the man's thrashing all but stopped.

"I . . . gaaah!"

"What?" said Slocum through clenched teeth.

"I . . . giiiive!"

"Damn right you do!"

JAKE LOGAN

SLOCUM
AND THE BIG
TIMBER TERROR

J

JOVE BOOKS, NEW YORK

THE BERKLEY PUBLISHING GROUP
Published by the Penguin Group
Penguin Group (USA) LLC
375 Hudson Street, New York, New York 10014

USA • Canada • UK • Ireland • Australia • New Zealand • India • South Africa • China

penguin.com

A Penguin Random House Company

SLOCUM AND THE BIG TIMBER TERROR

A Jove Book / published by arrangement with the author

For information, address: The Berkley Publishing Group,
a division of Penguin Group (USA) LLC,
375 Hudson Street, New York, New York 10014.

ISBN: 978-0-515-15491-7

PUBLISHING HISTORY
Jove mass-market edition / October 2014

PRINTED IN THE UNITED STATES OF AMERICA

10 9 8 7 6 5 4 3 2 1

Cover illustration by Sergio Giovine.

1

Pellets of snow drove at John Slocum's bearded face as he reined the Appaloosa to a halt. Squinting from under the low-pulled brim of his snow-caked fawn hat, he searched the darkening gloom for shelter of any sort. The grainy snow had built up over the past hour until the horse, normally a steadfast beast, had slowed his pace to a walk. The thick, dense snow had risen above the horse's knees, and Slocum knew they had to stop before the elements claimed them.

Off to their right, Slocum spied a dark-shadowed stand of pines. It would have to do. He tugged the reins and tapped heels to the tired horse's barrel, urging it toward the dark copse. They'd made it halfway from the narrow mountain road to the trees when a haunting, piercing howl from somewhere ahead halted them, tensing man and horse as if a snow-caked statue.

"What in the hell . . ." A low growl leaked out between Slocum's snow-crusted lips, a wisp of smoky breath pluming into the stormy sky. Didn't sound like a wolf, definitely not a coyote or a mountain lion. This was big, bellowing, throaty . . . like he imagined that giant ape would sound, the one that had been painted on the traveling circus banner he'd seen back in the flatlands of Wyoming the previous summer.

The sound echoed again, louder this time, and closer, now off to the left. Two of them? He held the Appy still, both man and horse nosing the chill air, scanning as far as they could see. The sounds dissipated into the freezing air, then no more noise came. They resumed their plodding walk to the stand of pines.

Sometime later, Slocum sat hunched in his sheepskin-lined mackinaw, stinging snow hurtling in all directions just beyond his campfire's struggling flames, pushed and pulled with every errant gust. Despite the stormy night, Slocum knew the crazy, every-which-way blasts could be much worse, were much worse, just a few feet beyond the mouth of his hastily constructed safe haven in the pines.

Deeper into the thicket of low-hung branches, laden with insulating, wind-blocking snow, the Appaloosa stallion seemed content to stand hipshot and head lowered, well out of the wind, his back still steaming from the last few hours of hard-put effort spent in getting them that far into the mountains.

Slocum had cleared a spot in the snow for the horse, and tied on a nose bag and let the horse eat while he cleared his own space and nursed a fire into something he might cook on. Despite the weather, and because of his somewhat decent campsite, he had increasing thoughts of making a warm meal, something he'd not indulged in for the past five days on the trail. The weather had been uncooperative and he'd been just tired—or lazy—enough at the end of the day that he didn't want to put in the extra effort cooking required.

But tonight, he had lip-licking thoughts of flapjacks, or maybe he'd fry up some bread, heat up some frijoles in a can until they bubbled, followed by a few cups of scalding black coffee. Nothing like it. He even had a couple of apples left over from their last visit to a mercantile. He'd split one with the horse as an after-dinner treat.

He set about heating the small, much-used enamel fry pan he carried with him, along with the much-battered coffeepot. These were motions he'd run through an untold number of times before, so much so that he suspected he could prepare a simple campfire meal without much thinking about it. For some reason, this journey found him in an increasingly ruminative mood.

As the storm whistled and waged, piling up then blasting away drifts of pearly, granular snow, Slocum bent to the task at hand of preparing the ingredients of his simple hot meal, secreted in this grotto-like spot in the trees. And as he did, he fell to musing about the course of events that had led him to this place, high in the Cascade Range in Oregon.

It had all begun with that thick-rumped stable girl outside Flintrock, Colorado. Darla had been her name—not an easy young woman to forget, she'd been more than a handful in every way. One of the less-than-ideal traits of being a long-time wanted man—for a crime that he shouldn't have been persecuted for—was that he had to always keep on the move, had to always keep one eye open, sleep with his trusty Colt Navy revolver close at hand.

Worst of all, he always had to move on just when he'd gotten to know interesting people. At most he had become reasonably assured over the years that he could take on ranch jobs for a season. And he liked signing on to a trail drive. The work was tough—long days eating dust, long hours in the saddle, and drinks and women few and far between. But the pay was decent if he signed on with the right outfit, and it most often kept him well away from the usual assortment of busybodies, bounty men, and boneheads he was likely to find in a town. Which suited Slocum to a T, as towns, except for the various conveniences they offered, had throughout his life offered little in the way of appeal. He'd rather camp in a blizzard, with high-country snow stacking up, than spend a week in a town in a soft bed. Well, most of the time.

But on this night in the mountains, he had fallen to thinking about Darla, the stable girl. He'd never learned her last name, only that she had inherited the stable from her husband, dead of a mule kick to the head a year or more by the time Slocum had wandered on into Flintrock, trail sore and looking for news about work.

It hadn't been difficult to find the livery stable—Darla's had been the only one in town. In fact, the town didn't have much to offer other than a collection of one of each. Slocum had joked with himself that the place should have been called One-ville. There had been one hotel—a run-down rattletrap of a place—one saloon, one mercantile . . . one one one. The saloon had even had one narrow-eyed, too-thin woman who Slocum thought had looked more like a schoolmarm than a soiled dove.

He had arrived there a couple of weeks before, during an unusually warm stretch of weather that everyone knew was odd and due to change soon. But they had all, Slocum included, enjoyed the late Indian summer sort of weather.

Darla had been impressed with his Appaloosa when he'd ridden into Flintrock that day. And Slocum had been impressed with her. Specifically with how she handled the horse. The Appy was prone at times to being ornery around strangers, and wasn't usually fond of women getting too close to him—not a trait that Slocum shared with his horse, thankfully. But the rugged girl, dressed in men's denims and a too-large flannel shirt that had seen much in the way of mending—all patches on the shirt and trousers had been done by a neat, precise hand—was a different sort of woman in most every way, once he got to chatting with her. After he saw her work, Slocum realized that was just Darla's way. For a big girl, she was tidy and seemed precise in all she did.

Little did he know, however, that not everything she did was careful and measured. Later that first night, not finding the hotel much to his liking, Slocum had asked her if she would mind if he bedded down in the empty stall beside his horse, the livery being less than full. Had it ever been full? he wondered.

"Not a problem," she'd said. By that time she had knocked off work for the day and he'd found her out back, sitting in a wooden chair with her boots off and her feet up, sipping a tall glass of well water and shielding her eyes as she watched the day's last rays of sun shrink down below the western skyline.

"Join me if you'd like, Mr. Slocum." She smiled then, a wide, honest, cheek-bunching smile, and patted the arm of a second wooden chair. "I can't offer much more than a cool glass of water, but the views are heartwarming enough, don't you think?" She'd looked at him without guile and winked, actually winked, but not in a lascivious way. In keeping with the attitude he'd seen earlier, the wink was that of one friend letting another in on a secret joke.

"With this weather, a cool glass of water and a fine view are just about right, I'd say," said Slocum as he sat down in the vacant chair and stretched out his legs.

She wagged her bare feet atop the rickety old sawhorse she'd propped them atop. "Kick off your boots, rest your feet. Plenty of room!" She giggled then and Slocum did the same as he shucked his boots and let his feet join hers atop the sawhorse. It swayed and wobbled, but held.

As the sun inched down below the ragged ridgeline far to the west, the coming night brought chill air down off the mountains. Darla stood and stretched, her flannel shirt tight against her ample breasts, her nipples poking the fabric like little fingers. Slocum caught all this in a glance, looked away lest she see him peeking, but it was too late.

To his surprise, she smiled and, staring right at him, rubbed her arms. "I sure could use some heat."

Slocum stood, returning her bold eye-locking stare. "I'll get you a blanket, if you'd like."

"Only if you're made of wool, Mr. Slocum."

He didn't need any more hint than that.

She stepped forward. He wrapped his arms about her, and ran his hands briskly up and down her back, feeling the firm muscles beneath. She was no spring flower, but a full-bodied workingwoman. And one of her working hands made its way around the back of his neck and pulled his head down to hers. She mashed her lips to his, then her breath, surprisingly cold, as if the coolness of the well water had remained lingering in her mouth, rose from her throat. But it was quickly chased down by a coiling heat that tasted to him of a musky sort of cinnamon. And he liked it. Like the mulled wine he'd once had at a Christmas celebration at a ranch in Idaho, sweet and spicy, and after a few glasses, you wondered what you ever did without it before then.

Somewhere between the stable's open back door and the sweet-hay-scented stall they collapsed into, Darla had lost her shirt, and managed to peel Slocum's denims down past his backside, which she kneaded with her work-hardened hands as if he were bread dough. He vaguely wondered what she might do to other parts of him, but he was too distracted shuttling her backward while he fought to keep up with her darting tongue and searching lips, her breath ragged.

She collapsed on her back into the mounded hay with a grunt, followed by a throaty giggle. She lay there for but a moment, looking up into his eyes, then drew him down to her. She wiggled and squirmed beneath him, and he realized she was not trying to free herself but to work her way out of her denims.

For all her power—and it was substantial—John Slocum, a man well north of six feet tall and with a physique as if he had been formed out of river rocks, did all he could just to keep up with her. But it was worth every second.

Rarely had he spent time with such a frantic, but genuinely excited woman. And he appreciated every little yip and shriek and giggle as she positioned herself beneath him. He plunged in with a full, thick thrust, and she appeared to enjoy every gliding stroke. And then she gripped his bare shoulders, rolled quickly to her left, and before Slocum knew what was happening, she was on top of him, emitting a low, satisfied growl close to his face in the waning light. And then she proceeded to ride him hard for ten relentless minutes.

He kept up, but there were a few points when he was sure he was about to collapse and whimper "uncle." Then she rolled off him and they lay side by side panting in the chilly air, in the near dark on the sweet hay.

Her voice broke the silence. "Thank you, Mr. Slocum. I haven't had anything like that since my husband died."

"Glad I could . . . help."

"Oh, you did, sir. But I'm afraid I'm not quite finished. Not just yet."

He was about to protest when he felt her hand working him, coaxing him back to rigid life. She giggled and worked her way down his body, kissing, until she stopped and brought him to full life once more . . .

A few weeks later and Slocum now found himself in the midst of a high-country blizzard, smiling at the memory of that long, exhausting, but excellent evening, and wondering why on earth he hadn't just stayed on for a few more days in that otherwise unremarkable little town of Flintrock. He grasped the hot handle of the little fry pan in a gloved hand and slid it away from flame and onto a rock, snow and bacon grease spattering and sizzling together.

"Because she likely would have been the end of you, Slocum." He said this aloud to no one other than the still-munching Appaloosa and the howling, dark, stormy night.

The warm memory of that earlier night carried his smile right on through supper. And did not wane until he was on his second cup of piping hot coffee, too full for the apple, though he still considered fetching it for the horse. Then he heard the noise that he'd thought he'd imagined earlier. This time, however, it was all too real, and closer than ever.

As Slocum looked beyond the small fire's light toward the close darkness, what he saw there in the dark, above man height, chilled the blood in his veins. Hovering a good eight feet off the ground were two green glowing eyes, a good hand's length apart and angled inward, as if whoever it was were filled with a seething rage.

And just as quickly as they appeared—moments after the too-close guttural screeching howl, bearing elements of rusted steel grinding on rusted steel, of the horrific terror of a live animal being peeled apart, of a sadness and rage balled together and expressed by someone who doesn't know how to speak, of the foul offspring of a mountain lion and a grizzly bear gagging out its anger in the sounds—Slocum watched as the eye lights faded backward into the buffeting night's storm. Then the sounds, too, abated, as if whatever had made them had come to some decision. And that was when he noticed the smell—just a whiff of something powerful, slaughterous, and raw and hot, like spilled blood and hair and rank old meat and more—then the wind shifted and it was gone.

But the Appaloosa had smelled it, too. The horse surprised Slocum by standing stock-still, looking almost comical despite the situation, as he stared out over the nose bag.

And that was what worried Slocum. He'd seen and heard, felt, smelled things too strange for words in his time, and this was something like all those times but completely different, too. After a few minutes of standing still, too stunned to move, the horse began to fidget and nicker, to shake and stamp its feet. Slocum calmed the Appaloosa with soothing sounds and a fresh rubdown. It seemed to help, but not enough to wipe away the nervousness and fear he still saw in the great beast's liquid brown eyes.

Slocum melted more snow and snapped more close-by branches, toed up more deadfall wood, and vowed to drink enough coffee to keep awake as long as it took for his own nerves to stop jouncing.

He suspected that might take all night. But he was fine with that.

2

"The nerve of some folks! Tellin' me—me!—Jigger McGee, that I ain't never gonna be able to get to town and back in three days." The old man's reedy voice poked like a thin-bladed knife into the still-blowing morning air, crisp with cold and the promise of more to come. The driving snow of the night before had slowed, but the flakes were still piling up. The objects of his shouted attentions were his two horses, high-stepping well-shod Belgian-cross brutes, bearing the bulging musculature of draft animals.

He rode behind them, perched on a split-log rail, his lap and legs covered with a patchy fur robe, more skin than hair, and he gripped the thick strap-leather lines wrapped around his fur gauntlets. "That's it, boys! Take 'er like she was meant to be took! This trail's a hard bitch and we'll give her no quarter!" He loosed a long, wheezing laugh.

"Titus! Balzac! You listening to me? Those stumble bums up to camp won't know what hit 'em when we mosey on back, slick as deer guts on a pump handle, loaded with supplies and liquored up. That'd be me, not you—you understand? I can't have my boys boozin' on the job!" His long, cackling laugh spun upward on an errant shaft of breeze as a slip of yarn might in a windstorm.

It was the laugh that jerked Slocum's intent gaze from his wavering fledgling fire to glance up toward the north, the direction he would soon be headed—right after he'd availed himself of a pot of coffee and a warming breakfast. As far as his calendar was concerned—the one he kept in his head, and that was rarely off by more than a day   he was a couple of days ahead of the date he'd intended to report in to the logging camp, still a good ten or twelve miles north. He had only a crude map drawn by the foreman's nephew, the barman at the TipTop Saloon, in Timber Hills. He'd assured Slocum, as had a handful of others, some of them loggers themselves, that there had been a boom in lumber to points south along the Cali coast, so much so that the various logging operations up north were hiring.

And hearing that had been almost as nice as hearing a dove's soft cries of amorous intent. Almost. For no matter how little money Slocum found himself in possession of, no matter how much time had elapsed between paying jobs, his thoughts were never too far from time spent, or time that would be spent, with a woman.

But this cold morning, the caterwauling, even above the somewhat dissipated morning wind, reminded him of the godawful howls he'd heard the night before. "Not again . . ."

Apparently the Appaloosa thought the same thing, for he nickered and dumped a steaming pile of trail apples.

"You and me both," said Slocum, fixing his eyes on the trail to the north and the increasing sounds drawing nearer. But this didn't sound quite like the gut-churning caterwaul of the night before. He heard chains, the telltale clopping of hoofbeats, muffled somehow by snow, no doubt. Though he could see nothing yet, he knew it was coming, whatever it was—likely a team. He stood, poured himself a steaming cup of coffee, and walked the couple dozen yards back to the trail, kicking through the nearly knee-deep snow.

With a gloved hand, he pulled back the flap of his thick coat, and thumbed the rawhide thong keeper free of the Colt's hammer and let his hand hang loose. No sense not being ready. He was barely aware that he'd done so—as a wanted man, he learned long ago to leave nothing to chance. This heightened sense of caution had cost him friendships, jobs, potential trysts with fine women, but since he was still alive while a number of other men—and a few sage women, over the years—were six feet under, it led him to trust his instincts. He must be doing something right.

Presently he saw movement through the thick pines, heard the rustling and jangling of chains and the occasional rope of laughter from whoever was crazy enough to be out this early on a stormy morning, driving a team southward.

Yep, now he saw it was a team of massive pulling brutes, thick necks bulging and straining under bulky fitted harnesses, the two horses chestnut in color and topped with a steaming layer of snow.

"Ho there! Ho there, boys!" the fur-wrapped man's cries echoed down at Slocum, along with a light wash of snow spray from the great hair-fringed hooves that excitedly clomped to a begrudging halt, the horses' heads bowed, mouths champing, breath pluming into the morning air.

The teamster, perched atop the big log sledge, eyed Slocum through a slit in a hoar-frosted woolly scarf wrapping his head. Finally, just as Slocum was about to greet him, the man spoke. "Who be you? And more to the point, is that real coffee I smell?"

The man made no motion that Slocum could construe as threatening, and kept his mittened hands held tight to the wrapped lines, since the big brutes towing him seemed a mass of quivering muscle, on the verge of bolting down the trail. It struck Slocum as impressive that the slight figure above him could contain such power.

Slocum sipped his coffee, then held up the cup. "I'm the man who just made that pot of coffee." He nodded vaguely behind him, to where his small but robust fire still crackled. "You're welcome to a cup, if you have the time."

Since the man and team obviously were engaged in some sort of logging activity, Slocum hoped the man might at least offer him a bit of friendly advice as to where the Tamarack Logging Camp was located. Mostly he was happy to see a living soul up here in high-timber country after not having seen another human for several days of slow travel. Something about the cold—and if he had to admit it, the freakish noises of the night before—had gotten to him.

"Well, right neighborly of you to offer." The sprightly little man was already setting the long-handled brake and coiling the lines around it, chattering like a camp jay all the way.

"Fact is, I'd about kill my best friend's best friend for a cup of the real stuff. Been a long time up to camp and we've had nary a sniff nor a whiff of the stuff. 'Bout thin on other supplies, too. That's how come I'm headed downslope. On a dead run I am, too. Made a wager with the men, you might say. They don't believe I can make the run down to town for supplies and get back in time afore they starve. Course, that ain't likely to happen, what with the deer and other critters we been chewin' on."

He swung himself off the narrow rail on which he was balanced, hung out over the deep white snow off to the side of the trail, then dropped into it, plunging in up to his waist, still yammering, this time to his horses.

Smiling, Slocum led the way to the fire, kicking as much of the snow out of his path as he could so the shorter man might follow with less trouble. He fished his second tin cup out of a saddlebag and filled it with piping hot coffee. By the time he'd stood up from the fire, hot cup in hand, the man was nearly beside him. The stranger unwrapped the frost-crusted wool scarf to reveal a thin, patch-bearded face sporting mostly silver-white hair. Deep creases along his cheeks, around his mouth, and across his forehead seemed to surround the two glinting blue eyes.

Slocum realized with a start that this man was no youngster as he had assumed. But whatever life he lived—presumably one in and around the great logging camps of the Northwest—it agreed with him. The man's ruddy skin looked like leather stretched over a bone frame. Even under all that fur wrapping him, Slocum doubted the man carried a smidgen of fat—he looked to be made of bone and gristle, with an extra helping of grit, all topped with mischief. This man, Slocum could tell, was a genuine, bona fide character.

The little man thrust out one mittened hand for a shake, to which Slocum obliged. Though Slocum gave as good as he got, the small man's impressive grip was like iron.

"I'm Jigger McGee, rowdiest log roustabout this here country's ever seen. Normally I'm in the woods, bucking logs and scaling trees and making sure the girl-men I work with don't catch a sliver and cry too long."

"Pleased to meet you, Mr. McGee. I'm Slocum, John Slocum."

Before he could continue, Jigger cut in, taking the proffered cup of hot coffee. "I bet you're up here sniffing for work. Am I right? Course I'm right. Nobody other than a fool or a logger'd be found up here any time of year, much less in a raging blizzard!" He sipped from the cup, wincing as he pulled in the steaming draught.

"You have it about right, Mr. McGee. I was in Timber Hills a few days back. The man behind the bar at the TipTop Saloon said the Tamarack Logging Camp, up this trail somewhere—"

The little man's mouth took on a sour, pinched shape.

"Coffee not to your liking?" said Slocum.

"Was . . . until you mentioned that barkeep. That little rascal is a thorn in the backside of every respectable logger in these parts. Been that way since the day he was whelped, so help us."

"How's that?" Slocum sipped his coffee, eyeing the curious little man.

"You sure ask a lot of questions, young fella."

"I wasn't aware I had exceeded my limit. Do you happen to know the way to the Tamarack?"

"There you go again, asking fool questions!"

"Why was that one foolish?"

"Because I'm from the Tamarack, just a few miles up yonder. Yep, that's where I come from. What do you think I been yammering on and on about since I got here?" The old man let loose with a long, slow sigh, shaking his head at the same time.

Slocum couldn't help cracking a smile. He hid it behind his cup and decided to change tactics. "At the risk of you thinking I'm some sort of crack-minded fool . . ."

That got the man's attention. He paused, eyebrows raised above the rim of his cup.

"I'd like to ask you about what I heard last night."

"Oh? And what would that be?"

"Well, that's the difficult part. I don't know what it was, but I can tell you it wasn't like anything I'd ever encountered."

"Well, out with it, mister!" Jigger growled.

Slocum regretted bringing up the subject. But he'd come too far with the silly story to back up now. "It sounded like a great howling bear crossed with a mountain lion crossed with a man—and a whole lot worse and angrier than all of them combined, too."

McGee's entire demeanor changed immediately, much

to Slocum's surprise. The old man leaned in close to Slocum and, looking around, said in a low voice, "You get a smell of it, too?" Before waiting for a response, he continued on chattering: "Reason I ask is that you ain't the first. Nor likely to be the last. It's a . . ." He leaned even closer. "A skoocoom, I tell you." The last part came out as barely a hissed whisper through his tightly clenched teeth.

"A what?" Slocum wasn't sure he'd heard the man right. If he had, then he knew the old-timer might be pulling his leg. For he knew what a skoocoom was supposed to be—a big, hairy, wild man of the woods. He'd heard the Indian tales. But that was pure hokum, even though the thought had occurred to him the night before. And then he thought of those eyes, bright and glowing green-yellow, and looking for all the world like something that couldn't possibly exist. But they had; that much he knew.

He came back to himself and saw the old man smiling at him, nodding, and then he winked. "You know what I'm talking about, sure you do. You know just what ol' Jigger's on about. Ain't too many folks in these parts would admit it but loggers and fools. And them are one in the same, so it was most definitely a skoocoom." He downed the last of his coffee, smacked his lips, and tossed the cup to the snow by the fire. "I best get going. I have a bet to win and a whole bunch of whining lumberjacks to make fools out of. And palavering with you ain't getting my work done, Mr. Slocum."

With that, the man started swaddling his head with the big wool scarf once again. Before he wrapped it around his mouth, he said, "Just follow this trail up to where I come from. You can't miss my boys' tracks." He nodded toward the now snow-covered team. Their body heat had cooled enough that the lightly falling snow laid a fine blanket on their backs.

"Obliged for the directions, Mr. McGee." Slocum stuck out his hand and the old man gripped it once again with his firm mittened claw hold.

"Call me Jigger. Any man who shares his coffee—even if it was godawful—and admits to seeing a skoocoom is set down in my book as a trustworthy sort."

Slocum wasn't aware he'd actually admitted anything other than hearing a strange noise.

As the little man plunged through the snow back toward his team, he shouted over his shoulder, "And tell 'em Jigger sent you. It's more than directions you got, it's a job from me, the camp boss!" He let loose a long, thin laugh, which peeled apart in a sudden gust of wind that obscured him from Slocum's view for a few seconds.

By the time the snow dust blew by, Jigger was seated on his rail-thin seat high on the great log sledge and adjusting the lines on his mittens.

"Ha, Titus! Ha, Balzac! Get up now! Get up there!" And the great team lunged into motion, their muscles straining and bulging as the sledge slid by, cutting a broad path on the snow-filled trail.

Slocum gave the cackling little man a stout wave and a nod, and wondered what had just happened, smiling and even whistling in the snowy morning as he went about the quick business of breaking his meager camp and saddling the Appaloosa.

3

By the time Slocum made it to Tamarack Camp, the snow-storm had dwindled to a light spitting, and veins of blue sky cracked the low raft of clouds. With it, a pressing feeling of dread mounted in Slocum's mind until he was sure he was being dogged by an unseen force lingering, tracking him from the woods. It was silly, he knew, and he wasn't normally a man given to superstition or feelings of unease, but damn, if this didn't raise the hairs on the back of his leathered neck.

A couple of times he swore he heard muffled thumping and occasional crashing, as if someone or something were following alongside him but well into the woods. Though every time he stopped, the whumping and barely detectable harsh breathing sound would stop, too, and Slocum saw nothing, despite swiveling fast in the saddle. Even the Appa-loosa perked his ears up, his eyes wide and his breathing more forced, as if he'd worked much harder than he had. Slocum kept his coat open, the Colt unthonged and ready to draw.

He sighed—there wasn't much he could do about it now. Especially since he could see the long log buildings, crouched dark and low against the snow like annoyed beasts waiting to be fed. Gouts of thick wood smoke curled upward into the brightening sky. Slocum knew breakfast would have, hours before, come and gone, and the men would be back in the woods, working away at making trees into logs.

Going on the trail had been slow. The deep snow, though granular, had forced the Appaloosa to high-step his way forward. Now that they approached the camp at last, Slocum felt that earlier sense of dread dwindling down to a thin line of worry. And that, too, pinched out with each step toward the one log shack, of the six in the cluster, with packed trails leading to it.

Usually that meant the cook shack, often a separate building from the sleeping quarters in these larger camps— or at least connected by a shade porch to the camp boss's quarters. And although he seemed like a crazy old coot, the boss in this camp was none other than Jigger McGee himself.

"Ho there!"

The voice had come from somewhere off to Slocum's right, back behind what he had thought was a big drift of snow. But that was only what it appeared to be. In truth, now that he had drawn closer, he saw it was a snow-topped log pile slowly being whittled down into stove-length chunks. And probably by the person who'd shouted at him.

A stocking-capped head, red and white stripes topped with a red pom-pom, poked up from behind the snow. The sun, just now glinting off the snow, made it difficult for Slocum to see the man's face, but he swore he was being eye-balled from beneath that funny hat.

"What you doing? Who you looking for?"

The voice bore an accent, probably French—a good guess since Slocum knew that most of the loggers in the Northwest region above and below the border were of French descent, many of them *voyageurs*—French trappers—turned loggers, at least for part of the season. It had to be a long, lonely life they led, but then again, Slocum mused, his wasn't so much different. He traveled somewhat with the seasons, took his work where he could get it before moving on.

Slocum tugged the brim of his fawn hat low over his eyes, a futile effort to cut the bright glare slanting in. "I'm here for work."

"Oh?" The hat disappeared. An axe rose up then came down hard. With a thunking sound. A few seconds later a man emerged, similar in height to Jigger, but broader of shoulder and obviously younger, given his full, bushy black beard and ruddy red face. He also carried an ample paunch, over which was spread a soot-and-food-stained apron that had at one time been white.

"Who be you, then?" said the man, striding straight toward Slocum on the well-trammeled snowy yard.

Slocum swung down from the Appaloosa. "I'm Slocum, John Slocum, and I was told down in Timber Hills that there was need of workers up here at the Tamarack Camp."

"Well now, mebbe *oui*, mebbe *non*."

"What's that mean?" said Slocum, offering a wry half smile.

The Frenchman nodded while he pulled out a stump of a pipe and clamped it in a corner of his mouth, jammed a thick thumb into the bowl, and worked whatever was in there with a vigorous motion before dragging a match across the stained apron and setting the pipe's contents alight. "You were told by someone to come here then?"

"Yep, that's what I said." Slocum thought for a moment, then figured, what the heck, give it a go, and said, "I also ran into a fellow name of Jigger McGee on the trail. Told me to come on up."

The effect of Jigger's name on the Frenchman's face was as if someone had conjured a magic trick. It brightened his glowering, drawn, black brows, and Slocum was sure there was a smile hidden somewhere in the thick bush of the man's beard.

"Well, why didn't you say so?" The man advanced and stuck out a burly hand. "Any friend of dat boss of ours is a good man, eh? I am Emil D'Artagnuile, but most folks call me Frenchy!"

I wonder why? thought Slocum, smiling. "Pleased to meet you, Frenchy."

Within minutes, Frenchy was giving Slocum a quick tour of the log-and-snow camp. They conversed from the start as old friends, chatting all the while as Slocum stabled the Appaloosa, watered and fed him, and lugged his gear to the bunkhouse.

"Frenchy, if Jigger's the boss, why was he headed to town on a supply run on his own?"

The Frenchman looked at him as if he'd stuck a grimy hand into the stewpot. "You tink dat's any of your business, Slocum?"

"Nah, in fact, I don't much care. I'm just making conversation." The last thing he wanted to do was ruffle feathers on his first day on the job. Especially those of a man built like a brick shithouse.

To his surprise, Frenchy looked left, then right, even though it was plain to see they were alone in the breezy outdoor cooking area between buildings. "Between you and me, the boss, he don't like nobody much to know his business."

"But everybody does anyway, I'll bet."

"You gonna let me talk, or are you gonna run your mouth like a steam engine?"

"Go ahead, Frenchy. I'm all ears."

"Good. So I was thinking that maybe you was one of them chatty fellas who talks and talks but don't say nothing and everybody finally gets tired and . . ."

He kept on prattling while Slocum nosed about the small covered cooking space. The big black stove formed almost the entire back wall. From the looks of the behemoth, it gobbled a hell of a lot of wood just to keep the loggers fat and happy. Even now, at roughly ten o'clock in the morning, the sides were working up to a steady orange glow.

"So anyways, like I was saying to you, Slocum, the boss, he has other reasons for going to town on his own. But don't you worry." Emil wagged a gleaming steel spatula in Slocum's face. He knew the Frenchman didn't mean anything by it, but anyone else and he'd likely have lost a limb by now. Slocum decided to let it pass. He wanted to hear the reasoning behind Jigger's solo trek, despite it being one of those things that seemed amiss about the operation.

In fact, since he'd heard of the Tamarack Camp back in Timber Hills in the bar, there seemed more questions about it than answers. Why was the Tamarack the only camp not filled with loggers at this late date in the season? What was it doing advertising in a bar? Why did the bartender seem to know so much about the camp's business?

And oddest of all, what was the camp boss, Jigger McGee, doing riding herd on a big ol' team down to town for supplies when such a chore was usually reserved for a teamster? Seemed like the camp boss would want to be around to tend to his men and oversee the operation of the camp. Slocum didn't give voice to any of these concerns; he figured he already had done enough of that.

"I tell you what, though." Frenchy dropped a dollop of grease into a bubbling vat of stew. "Jigger, he's a man who knows his business. He knows logs like I know biscuits." The big man smiled wide. "And I cook a good biscuit. You will know soon."

Slocum was about to ask him if Jigger was part owner of the Tamarack when Frenchy continued talking.

"But there's something wrong with things here. Has been for some time."

It was almost as if Frenchy were talking to himself as much as, or more than, he was addressing Slocum.

"What's that?"

"Dere you go again, interrupting Frenchy." The burly cook shook his head and kept talking. "I don't know the wrong of it, but I know at least that he has some money troubles. It ain't easy keeping this camp going."

That answers my unspoken question about Jigger being owner, or at least part owner, of the Tamarack Camp, Slocum thought.

"But the log sales are good now, so he went maybe to make deals? Maybe to visit his daughter in town, *non*?" Frenchy shrugged and fell silent, rummaging on a dusty shelf packed with spice tins and jars.

"What can I do to help, Frenchy?"

The man spun on him. "Oh yes, you are here to work! Not listen to Frenchy talk and talk, *non*?" Again the big man laughed, then said, "I hope you can swing an axe, mister. I have a powerful need for, how you say, *beaucoup*"—he spread his hands wide, his big wooden spoon dripping stew juice on the wood floor—"split firewood, eh? Lots and lots. Come, I'll show you to the woodpiles."

"Well, what in hell do we have here?"

Slocum turned to see a seedy, rail-thin man, all bone and gristle, with a narrow, wedge-shaped face, in the middle of which was pinned the bulbous red-ended nose of a heavy drinker. Small, too-close eyes topped it, and regarded Slocum with a squinty stare and a half smirk, as if he were looking at a bug he was about to render flat with his hobnailed boot.

Slocum had seen this very sort of wormy apple in a hundred cow towns, mining camps, and frontier settlements, and they never changed much. He wondered vaguely if they all came from the same place, sort of like a storeroom somewhere in the back alleys of Saint Louis. He could picture them emerging at dusk from the bowels of a great, sagging, sodden warehouse along the river, all looking roughly the same. That is to say, they all would look ratlike, spineless, seedy, stupid, and desperate. But most of all, dangerous.

"What's so funny, kitchen boy?"

Slocum guessed he himself must have been smiling at the thoughts he'd conjured of this fool and all his ilk. He didn't respond, just sighed and rested a hand on the end of his double-bit axe.

"I said—"

"I heard you."

Rat-face stepped closer, two long, bony thumbs hooked in the waistband of his green wool trousers held up by brown leather braces. His shirt nearly completed the traditional logger's garb in these parts—a red-and-black-checked wool affair topping familiar pink-tinged longhandles that before long wear and many washings had begun life as red longhandles.

Atop the man's head was perched a variation on the same toque Frenchy wore—a knitted wool topper—but this one was black and lacked the decorative pom-pom.

"Then why don't you answer to me when I speak?"

Slocum sank the axe into the chopping block and faced the man. Rat-face's smirk slumped a mite, and he swallowed back what Slocum was sure was a knot of regret big as a peach pit and going down mighty tough. And he knew why.

Without feeling boastful of it, Slocum knew he appeared a formidable figure to some men. In addition to his superlative skill with a gun, and being better than fair with a knife, he was also deadly when he had to be with his bare knuckles. He had been able to rely on all these skills in dodgy situations over the years. Indeed, he had always had a somewhat imposing size, at well above six feet, and with nary a wasted pound of fat on him. He was muscle and bone, wide of shoulder, and looked as if he'd been chiseled from granite.

"Let's get this straight," said Slocum, slipping his own wool shirt back on over his muscle-tight longhandle shirt. "You are trying to tell me when and to whom I should speak. Now is that right? Can you possibly be telling me such a thing?"

"Sure he is." And along from out behind the log pile came another rough-looking character. This one was a fleshy-faced man, dressed enough like the other man that most anyone could tell they were loggers.

He looked to be a little taller, maybe a little wider at the shoulder and heavier in the hand. But they both shared that desperate look, as if they felt the world owed them something and they'd decided to take everything they could in return. Even if it was nailed down.

The second man's appearance swelled the first man's chest enough that he regained some of his smirk and nodded. "Yeah, that's right. And—"

"And what, big boy?" said Slocum, rolling up his cuffs.

"Uh, um . . ."

The second man shifted a quid of chaw to his other cheek. "He said that you guessed right. Now tell the man who you are and what you been up to, what you aim to get up to."

"Why should I?" said Slocum, his neck muscles flexing with each biting pulse in his jaw. Then the two men advanced on him and a thought occurred to him at the same time. And he smiled. "Oh," he said, steadying himself. "All right, then."

The two men strode up fast, the burlier one in the lead, Rat-face coming in close behind. Slocum could see their clenched fists, guessed that the lead man was an experienced brawler, judging from the scar tissue veining his homely face and the knobbed knuckles on his broad hands.

The lead man came in quick, almost quicker than Slocum expected. Almost. As Slocum let the man take the first swing, a round-houser sloppily thrown by someone who assumed he was going to land a hard hit, Slocum side-stepped. "I'll tell you what I'm about to get up to, since you insist."

He pivoted on his left leg, snaked his muscled torso outward, then back in just after the lead man followed his own poorly thrown punch. Instead of driving a hard fist into the retreating side of the man's face, he let the fool's own momentum work for him and drove the heel of his palm hard against the meat of the man's shoulder. It wouldn't render him immobile, but Slocum knew it would buy him time enough to get ready for Rat-face.

The driven palm-to-the-shoulder did the trick and sent the buffoon sprawling face-first to the packed surface already covered with bark chunks, boot grime, churned muck, and sopping, slushy snow. The combination greased the man's sprawl and sent him skidding a good six feet before he flopped and grunted to regain his feet.

In the meantime, Rat-face had surprised Slocum—and probably himself—by howling like a schoolgirl and launching himself straight at the brawny newcomer. He made the mistake of lowering his head and making a bull run straight at Slocum. He must have forgotten what a weak man he was, for his head did indeed connect with Slocum's midsection, but as it was a plank of ribbed muscle, Rat-face's neck bent and folded under himself. He curled up like a stunned kitten, a ball of wool and quivering limbs at Slocum's feet.

His heaving chest and a strangling whimper told Slocum the man was at least alive, if not neck-broke. He toed the man onto his back and let him gasp, face up.

The lead man stood some feet away, hands on knees, heaving, blood and grit smearing his homely features, muck pasted to his shirtfront. "What did you do to him?" The bloodied man nodded toward the wreck at Slocum's feet.

"I didn't do a thing to him." Slocum gestured downward. "He did all this himself." He looked at the lead man. "Talented fella, isn't he."

Slocum forgot how much vim and vigor the average logger had, and this one proved no exception. The man rose up from his bent position, a wide, bloody leer of raw rage stretched across his foul face, and he, too, ran full bore at Slocum. He wasn't as ruggedly built as Frenchy, but the man had boldness and power, and he used them in a quick combination that drove Slocum backward, catching him before he could steel himself or, better yet, sidestep again.

But as dumb as he looked, it seemed as if the lead man at least had the ability to learn from his mistakes. He anticipated that Slocum might sidestep his charge, and at the last second he altered his course, driving his left shoulder hard into Slocum's side. The blow caught Slocum off guard and drove him backward, his left knee collapsing. He hit the wet churned ground hard, sending up a spray of slush.

It took him but a moment to recover and wrap a meaty arm around the attacker's stiff-muscled neck. He wrenched it tight, made to grab his wrist with his free hand, but the man had already begun to buck and twist out of his hold.

Slocum balled his free hand's fist and drove it down hard at the man's face—not because it was the easiest or best course of action at that point, but because in the flash of a second, he'd seen the man lunging with his mouth, trying to bite Slocum's encircling forearm.

He would not abide a man who bit another man. That was child's play, not proper fighting. His fist connected hard with the man's cheek and nose, made a crunching, snapping sound as it hit. Slocum felt the nose smear sideways under his knuckle, and it felt good, considering the nonsense these jackals had doled out, and all without knowing him.

The man continued to snap his stumpy teeth, squirm, and now gurgle on his own blood, but he didn't stop his thrashing attack. He was frenzied, so Slocum gave him another hard drive to the face. This one landed above the man's cheekbone. Slocum had had enough experience in the manly art of pugilism to know that his punch had delivered the ingredients of a black eye to the rascal. He'd wake up tomorrow with a throbbing blue, purple, and yellow shiner.

That blow slowed the man's writhing to a random but weakened struggle. Soon, and with a little more help from Slocum's tightening arm, the man's thrashing all but stopped.

"I . . . gaaah!"

"What?" said Slocum through clenched teeth.

"I . . . giiiive!"

"Damn right you do!" Slocum gave him a hard thrust and rolled the bloodied and bludgeoned mess of a man from atop him, then stood, smoothing the wet grime from him. He didn't have too much more in the way of clean dry clothes in his war bag, but at least he knew where there was a hot stove.

As if beckoned, Frenchy appeared, meaty hands on his hips, apron even more soiled than it had been less than an hour before when Slocum had left him to his meal prepping chores. "*Mon Dieu!* What has happened here?"

"Ask those two," said Slocum, nodding toward the flopped, heaving men on the ground.

"But you bested the two of them?"

"Yeah, not proud to say one of them got the drop on me, though."

"But this has not happened before!" Frenchy sidled up close to Slocum, spoke low. "They are, how you say, bad eggs. They are not from here, but they have the ears of some of the men of the Tamarack Camp. You see?"

"No, I don't really see, but I suspect I'll get the lay of the land pretty soon." Slocum slid off his wool shirt and shook it.

"But you don't understand, Slocum," said Frenchy, glancing at the two men, who were just beginning to groan loudly, almost in unison, and beginning to show signs they might stand within an hour or so.

"Frenchy, pardon me for saying so, but they're the ones who attacked me, right? So why are you so afraid? Can't be you're afraid of them, are you?"

"I . . ." He looked again at the men. The skinny one fixed Frenchy with a hard stare while he gingerly rubbed his neck.

"I must go, Slocum." He turned to walk away, then swung back quickly and said, "Tread with care, you hear me? If not for your sake, then for the sake of Jigger, *non*?" Then he headed back toward the cook shack, cutting a wide circle around the two rogues. In a louder voice, over his shoulder, he said without looking back, "You had better shape up, Slocum, and get that firewood ready, or you will find yourself without a job, *oui*?"

Well, thought Slocum, as the English girl said in Wonderland, this thing just keeps getting curiouser and curiouser. He draped his wool shirt on the jutting butt end of a log, then slipped his gun belt and Colt Navy off another log end and strapped them on. He stepped around the chopping block, keeping it between him and the two moaning men. He wasn't quite sure what to do with them, since according to Frenchy, they weren't Tamarack men. So who were they? Once they came to, he decided he'd ask, knowing full well they'd not share a thing with him. As he set to splitting stove lengths again, he ruminated on what an odd situation it was that he'd willingly ridden into.

Wouldn't be the first time, he told himself. Nor the last, he guessed.

4

"There was a time when I would have kicked your ass, boy. You understand me? That time has long since come and gone, though."

That night in the dining hall, the man speaking eyed Slocum from beneath two bushy eyebrows that looked like a pair of haired-up caterpillars about to duke it out. The aging logger set down his tin coffee cup and smiled. "But I reckon I'll let you live today."

The crowded dining hall had just about quieted down right before the old man spoke. But when he did begin speaking, the remaining din dropped to almost nothing and all of the rangy, beard-faced men swung their heads in his direction. Once he spoke, from the barely concealed smirks on their faces, Slocum knew the older fellow was pulling his leg.

Why, he had to be—he didn't look like he could do much more than rassle an unconscious raccoon. But Slocum had been in enough ranch cook shacks, dining messes, and cow camps to know about a bit of joshing of the new man in camp. And this little tirade by the old man had all the ear-marks of it.

Problem was, and Slocum knew he had to temper his outlook a mite, those fellows from earlier had at first seemed like they might be up to the job of taking him down, but they hadn't. Still, he'd been the one to pay for it.

They had up and skedaddled by the time he'd returned from bringing a load of firewood to Frenchy's kitchen, so he never got the chance to quiz them about who they were working for and why in the hell they had attacked him. Though he was pretty sure it was just a case of ribbing the new arrival, Slocum was nonetheless skittish.

"What you say to that, Slocum?" said Frenchy, hauling in yet another platter of hot elk steaks, sawed off the frozen carcass just that afternoon—Slocum knew because he'd helped with the task.

He set his fork and knife down across the chipped enamelware plate, raked his callused fingers through his thickening beard. He was glad he hadn't shaved weeks back, and even gladder when he had stayed his razor hand just an hour before he found out back in Timber Hills about the potential logging job.

Not only did having a beard help keep the cold air away from his face, but showing up in camp with a decent set of whiskers made him seem less of a greenhorn to these woods-hardened men. Each one of them had been seasoned in the frosty pitch and thundering crashes of old-growth pines. They took them down with whipsaws, then stood back as the long carcasses of the big brute trees thundered down to the frozen earth, raking the hell out of anything in their path on the way down, before slamming flat anything that was dumb enough to stay rooted beneath them as they fell.

"I tell you what . . . *old-timer.*" Slocum let that remark hang in the air for a few moments. It stung the old buck—

that much was for certain. Slocum flicked his eyes toward the graying gent, whose smiling face bunched into a tight pucker, his dark eyes glinting for a few seconds. Until the glances of the other men settled on him, that is. Then he let a slow grin spread wide on his face.

That was a relief to Slocum. He was tired of games today, dog-tired from having to dole out significant fisticuffs to those two morons, and triple-tired from the quantity of stove lengths he'd split all day. Even Frenchy himself had marveled at the massive mound of raw split wood Slocum had managed to get through.

"Never has no one sized it up quite so fast as you, Slocum," the portly cook had said, rubbing his paunch with an appreciative hand, his other scratching in his beard as if looking for remnants of snacks he'd stored there earlier.

Slocum had wanted to work hard, to exercise his body, his one most reliable weapon—besides his well-oiled Colt Navy, that is. He always tried to take care of himself that way, and was rarely let down by some failing of it. He'd seen countless gunmen and ranchers, cowboys, and drifters who'd all let their bodies go to seed, who'd trusted in the powers of youth, trusting blindly that the bodies of their youth would never wane, only to be let down at a crucial moment.

And now he was dog-bone-tired and not looking for another round of fighting, real or imagined.

"I would say, old-timer, that you have the right to believe whatever it is you want. But know this." Slocum held up a cautionary finger. "If there's one thing that many a man has tried to do, it's best me in a round of hard pit-fighting. And while some of them have done so, it hasn't been pretty for either side. Not bragging much, mind you, just a simple fact." All the while he said this, he smirked, knowing he was teasing the old man before his cohorts, and knowing that they all knew it, too.

Slocum always tried to keep in mind one thing his long-dead father had once told him: "You can say anything you want to about anyone you want to, John, as long as you say it with a smile on your face and a twinkle in your eye. Friend, enemy, or in between, it doesn't matter much. Just have at it—with a smile, that is."

The entire dinner, once he proved that he could take what they dished out and even dish a heaping helping right back to them, was a pretty favorable affair, all things considered. They were a bunch of good men out there to do a rough job, much the same as the men in a hundred cow camps and cow towns. For a while Slocum let himself slip into the genuineness of the camaraderie, the good-natured revelry that comes up in a group of hardworking men at the end of a long day's labors. It was a fleeting thing, he knew, just as it always was on trail drives and ranch jobs.

But he decided he would ride it out as long as he needed to. And considering the paltry state of affairs that was his wallet, he felt certain he'd need a whole lot more good days up here in the sticks just to climb back out of the money hole he'd recently found himself in. So he put up with it and soon learned about the forest in which they were working. It would be a busy winter season, made especially so by orders from the "Far Orient," as one young bookish logger put it.

Soon the talk flowed with the hot coffee, and though a number of men broke off in small groups to head to bed, others lingered by the stove, turning occasionally to redden the other sides of their faces, playing dominoes and cards with their fellows. Around the table a throng of men stayed, eager to talk about the woods they'd spent the entire day in.

Reminded Slocum of the cowboys who would linger in a stable or leave their bedroll early just to spend time with other cowboys, watching over the herd, talking horses, comparing notes about the terrain and weather.

He also noticed that the men appeared to be split unevenly

into two rough groups. One was filled with what he came to think of as the scowlers, the half of the men who didn't even bother offering him the pretense of a smile. They just sneered at him as if he were a disease-riddled bum. The others treated him with kind caution that looked to be fast breaking down into camaraderie once the conversation flowed.

It was curious and worth noting, he thought, that the men in neither group conversed much with those in the other. Not unusual in large groups of men, but given all the strangeness of the day, Slocum couldn't help wondering if this wasn't another in the seemingly unending series of oddities about the Tamarack Logging Camp.

"One thing you got to get straight in your head once you get out there," said a young climber named Ben, "is that them trees won't do much of what you ask 'em to. Oh, they all fall if you give 'em enough strokes to the trunk. But the key is to be on the safe side of the trunk when she starts to go!" The young man thought that was about the funniest thing he'd heard in quite some time, given the guffawing ruckus he made. The other men just rolled their eyes at the young man, obviously used to his odd sense of humor.

"Pay him no never mind, Slocum," said a salt-and-pepper-bearded man, not particularly tall or wide, but solid-looking, as if he were all bone and muscle, all hard worker. He plucked his stubby pipe from between his lips. "He's a pup, but he's good at what he does."

That made Ben blush and seemed to Slocum as good as telling him he was full of beans. A compliment paid among workingmen often had that effect.

The older, solid man drew on his pipe, let the smoke out in a leisurely stream, then continued. "Occurs to me we haven't asked Slocum what his experience in the forest has been."

Slocum couldn't help smiling. This was the one question

he'd be awaiting, and a little surprised that they hadn't yet asked him. All eyes swung to him, even the men closer to the stove, huddled over coffee, shuffling chipped dominoes and plinking checkers, darning their holey wool socks, or slapping down pasteboard cards. All activity paused. This was their chance to hear if the newcomer was a braggart, and to hear of his experiences. Unless, of course, he *was* a braggart.

Slocum knew all eyes were on him, so he chose his words carefully, chewed them like a good steak before speaking. Finally he said, "I don't have as much experience as most of you. But I have spent time swinging an axe on a couple of forest crews, have bucked plenty of board feet of lumber working at a sawmill, and have cut my share and then some of logs for cabins, though mostly for burning to keep ranch hands warm. No getting around that when you're working cattle country up high in the Northern Rockies. Those winters get cold."

"Never understood why cowfolks and such think they need to spread their cattle all over hill and yon." It was the old man again. "Keep 'em down in the low country, I say. Down where they can't bother a man making an honest living in the woods."

Slocum bristled slightly. "You saying working cattle is dishonest?"

The old man squinted through his pipe smoke. "Now I ain't saying no and I ain't saying yes. What I am calling into question is whether it's work at all." He drew once again on a pipe, a little too emphatically for Slocum.

Another test. But Slocum decided he'd been through enough that day and would let the old man have his fun another time. He certainly wasn't about to let the old buck goad him into a kerfuffle.

Before he could say as much, make his excuses, and head to the bunk Frenchy had assigned to him earlier, a gust of sudden wind rocked into the thick, log wall cabin, driving smoke back down the chimney. One man who had, moments before, announced he was bushed and was calling it a night had reached for the door handle when the gust hit.

The wind itself wasn't much of an event to cause concern, other than for someone to twist the damper handle on the stove pipe in an attempt to slow the backwash of smoke. But what followed it as if carried on the wind itself did raise everyone's eyebrows.

The long, plaintive wail, at once wolflike and human, did not pinch out but continued, building in depth and becoming a low guttural growl, snapping and harsh. Men from both unofficial groups whitened and widened their eyes. Slocum couldn't help feeling the same spine-freezing chill he'd felt the previous night, as if bony fingers of the long-dead were raking his backbone, tapping his scalp, ready to tighten around his neck.

The sounds dropped off instantly, replaced with another slamming gust of wind. Moments later the sounds of animal rage began again, closer to the cabin. The men were all riveted, watching the side of the cabin as if the very frosted log walls might explode inward at any second. Slocum fancied he heard footsteps crunching hard in the snow outside. He moved cautiously to the door, shucked his Colt Navy on the way, and laid a bare hand on the latch. The sounds abated and Slocum, listening to a flurry of whispered protestations, stayed his hand for a moment.

"Don't go out there, Slocum. Bad news."

"What do you mean by that?" he said in a low voice.

"I mean, it's the skoocoom, man!"

That was what Jigger had told him earlier, and the boss man had reacted in much the same way. But the skoocoom was a fairy story, nothing more. At least that was what he had believed up until last night. Then he heard that thing, saw those green-yellow eyes staring him down from the darkness outside his meager fire's circle of light. Now he was just plain confused about skoocooms. Doubly so since it seemed these Tamarack loggers actually believed in the creature.

But now that he was faced with it once again, he was determined to figure out what in the hell it was, despite being admittedly disturbed once again by the freakish sounds.

He swallowed deep, snatched up the bail of a lantern hanging on a hook from a ceiling beam, and wrenched the door inward. He held the lantern aloft before him and stood in the doorway a moment before venturing out onto the path worn in the snow.

He heard shuffling and the sounds of chairs squawking on floorboards as men jockeyed in a throng behind him. "Hold up there," said the thin, salt-and-pepper-bearded man behind him. "I'll go with ye. You men," he said to the rest, "don't go locking this door now. We'll make a circle around the building then be back afore you know it."

Slocum was relieved to have the company. The howls had stopped, but he recalled they had come from something that had drawn quite close to the side of the cabin. And since he'd never seen nor heard of anything that substantial not leaving sign or tracks behind, Slocum was determined to find evidence of it, be it beast or man.

5

Jigger McGee arrived in Timber Hills at dusk that night, as the sky purpled and the breaths of the few people hustling along the boardwalks plumed thick and hung, cloud-like, in the dense, stormy air.

"That you, Jig?"

"Who said that?" The small, wiry, fur-clad man spun on his hard rail of a seat behind the pair of mighty Belgians thundering slowly along the darkening street. Two streets north a dog barked, received no answer, tried again.

"You know damn well who it is, Jig." Out of the shadows stepped a squat man whose shadowed bulk spoke of great girth.

"Torrance Whitaker, I shoulda known it was you, wormin' around in the shadows." McGee dragged a cuff across his mouth and loosed a stream of tobacco juice. It spattered in a rough spot at the fat man's feet. The man didn't even finch, just kept his eyes on Jigger.

"And my nostrils should have told me it was you coming, McGee. Those foul horses of yours can be smelled from

39

clear across the county. And believe me when I tell you, that isn't a compliment." He waved a gloved hand before his face as if a terrible stench had infiltrated his nostrils.

"Nobody talks about my boys that way and lives it down. So shut your homely, fat face, Whitaker. Or I'll be glad to do the job for you."

"Now aren't you a defensive little fellow." Whitaker cast the remark out, but Jigger didn't rise to the bait.

"What do you want?" It galled Jigger to think that by asking, he was showing interest in what Whitaker had to say, but he couldn't help himself. The fact was, Jigger wanted to know just what Whitaker's plans were, precisely because the fat man was the biggest landowner in those parts, and a major thorn in Jigger's side. "I'm getting a little tired of you popping up anytime I make a trip to town."

"Well now," said Whitaker, puffing on a finger-thick cigar and doing his best not to shiver from the cold. "Seems to me you ought to be nicer to me. Especially considering I am the one and only person in the world who can make your life better than the living hell it currently is."

"How do you know what my life is like?" Jigger's voice rose in pitch, and a couple of men on the far side of the street looked up from their conversation.

"Let's just say that everyone knows what your life is like, Jig. And it isn't a pretty thought."

McGee sputtered and delivered a string of blue oaths, but Whitaker kept right on talking. "First there's the debt load you carry. Then there's the poor quality of the work your loggers deliver."

"What? *What?*" Jigger shook with rage and trembled as he looped the lines around the brake and prepared to jump down from the sledge.

Oddly enough, Torrance Whitaker held his ground and kept right on talking and puffing on his cigar. Despite the creeping cold temperatures, people began to leak out of the fog-windowed storefronts and saloons to hear what the shouting ruckus was all about. And they began to recognize the two combatants as right-full-of-himself, rich-as-sin Torrance Whitaker and Jigger McGee, a solid, if cantankerous, fellow liked by most who took the time to know him.

Whitaker puffed long on his stogie and glanced in appreciation at the growing crowd. "And then there's the fact that you have been late on your payments to the bank a few too many times, Mr. McGee."

That brought Jigger up short. "What are you saying? What business is my business to you? Hmm?"

"Considering I just guaranteed the bank's solvency in exchange for the presidency of said institution . . . " Whitaker thumbed his lapels and rocked back on his boot heels. "I'd say I have every right in the world to call into question your haphazard dealings. In fact, I'd go so far as to say you're a public menace to the fine society of Timber Hills."

It was Jigger's turn to smile, despite what he'd just heard. "What makes you say I'm a menace . . . President Whitaker?"

"Why, the very fact that you are, as we speak, in danger of defaulting on your loan puts the very life savings of everyone in our fair town at risk." He sucked in a full chest of air and said in a louder, booming voice, "At great, great risk."

Jigger reached into the foot space of his mighty sledge and pulled out a worn leather satchel, packed and strapped tight.

"What's that?" said the fat man, his cigar drooping between his chapped pink lips.

"This?" said Jigger, holding the bag aloft. "Oh, this ain't nothing much. Just a whole lot of cash." He leaned forward until the two men's faces were barely a foot apart, but he spoke loudly. "To make my bank payment in full and on time. Might even be some extra there, too, for next month."

"But how is that possible? I told—"

"You told Deke Tiffins not to buy my logs, is that it?"

The fat man spluttered, and even in the dim light of the street, folks could see him turning a rich hue of crimson. "I . . . I never . . ."

"You never what, Mr. President? You never told the truth in your life? Now that I'll believe. But you by gum sure did tell ol' Deke you were going to shut him down if'n he bought my logs. But you seemed to forget—or maybe you never knew, being an outsider and all—that me and Deke, we go *waaay* back. Come out here to this rugged old country together, in fact." He smiled as the fat banker's face puffed and wobbled.

Torrance Whitaker chewed his cigar as though it were a wad of jerky, but he could think of nothing to say.

"Next time you go to threatening a man, you best consider his friends, you hear?" Jigger McGee turned a beaming face on the assembled townsfolk, enjoying a smile at Whitaker's expense.

"Now, now, Jigger. I am, after all, only looking to provide my future daughter-in-law with a safe and secure future. A nest egg, if you will."

"What do I care how safe and secure your family is, Whitaker?" Jigger rasped a hand across his old curly wolf of a beard and turned toward the bank. "Way I see it, they can all go hang fire, for all I care."

Whitaker smiled slow and wide, puffed once, twice, pluming blue smoke skyward, then said, "Pity you feel that way about your own daughter, Jig. But then again, that doesn't surprise me. You're a selfish fellow, you know that?"

With that, Whitaker turned his back on Jigger, who still stood by the hanging heads of his boys, the Belgian team, and tried to raise something more than an agitated grunt. The sad part of hearing the news about his own beloved daughter was that he didn't really doubt what Whitaker had said about her becoming Torrance's daughter-in-law. So strained had their relationship become in recent months that he wouldn't put it past the girl to do that to him, in fact.

Finally Jigger, slump-shouldered, sighed long and low and hefted the leather satchel, the one thing he had been so proud of but a few moments before, but that now seemed so damned useless. He slowly walked down the street toward the still-glowing front window of the bank. "Let me down, just like her mother," he mumbled. As he headed for the bank, the wind picked up and felt like a slap to the face.

6

"Slocum, what are you doing with that light?" Ned, the wiry older man who ventured outside with him, gestured with his pipe at the snowy mounds before him. "There's something over here. Can't quite see what, though."

Slocum brought the lantern in low just as an errant gust filled in a track that at its bottom looked as though it had been made by a massive human foot, padded like a bear's, and tipped with great curving claws where the toes ended.

"You see that?" he said, shouting close by Ned's ear.

The other man merely nodded, then gestured onward ahead with his pipe stem. "More there. Best look at 'em before the wind fills them in, too."

In this fashion they made their way around the far end of the long, low, log structure. Occasionally from inside they could hear muffled words from the men, the occasional bark of laughter shushed by other more strident voices. There was something to this howling noise business, and Slocum was eager to find out just what it was that got all these burly loggers in such a worked-up state.

"We best get back inside," said Ned.

In the dark, the man's voice, close by to be heard over the whistling wind, startled Slocum. He jerked out of reflex. "Damn, Ned, you rattled me."

"Good," said the man, smiling and gesturing back toward their rapidly filling tracks. "Now you know how the rest of us feel. Even if those big goobers in there wouldn't admit it."

"Ned," said Slocum as they made their way back toward the cabin door. "What exactly do you think this skoocoom is anyway? As for me, I've heard it, last night and tonight. Hell, I even saw it."

The effect Slocum's words had on Ned was as if he'd yanked the man hard with a fishhook and line. "You saw it? Why didn't you say so? Tell me, what did it look like?"

"Hold on a second. I may have misspoke. I saw its eyes. Greenish-yellow glowing things about eight feet off the ground. I tell you what, in all my days on the trail, I've never seen a creature's eyes like that."

Ned nodded, but said nothing.

Just before they reached the door, from the opposite direction they'd just come, they heard the grating, cracking sound of wood being wrenched apart, coupled with the creature shrieks they'd heard earlier. But this time they were outside with it, whatever it was, and this time the sounds were louder, more violent and earnest in their howlings, and this time, they were doubled, as if made by two of the beasts.

"Lordy Lord . . . " said Ned. Even in the dim lantern light and the wind-driven swirl of pelting snow, Slocum could see that his companion had turned ashen-faced. The man looked to have aged tremendously in mere minutes.

Slocum wanted to investigate. No, he told himself. That's not quite true. What I want to do is go back in there in the warm cabin with the other loggers, sidle up to the fire, and wait it out. Herding instinct must have kicked in, though he tried to laugh it off. In truth, he was as scared—or perhaps more scared—than he had been the night before when he and the Appaloosa were alone in the hills.

The horse! Horrible thoughts of the beast attacking the Appy drove down on him. "Ned," he shout-whispered. "Where's that sound coming from? What building is it attacking? I don't have the lay of the camp yet."

"Oh hell, Slocum. We got to get the boys. That thing is tearing up the storehouse. One thing we can't take is losing our supply of vittles, our dynamite, all our necessaries!"

He was already pushing his way inside.

"Come on, Slocum, strength in numbers!"

But Slocum was already stepping into the darkness, his Colt still poised in his cold-stiffened left hand, the guttering lantern in his right. "No, I'll go on ahead. You gather the men, and let's get to the bottom of this." Snow stung his face, his hands throbbed from the cold, and he couldn't feel his feet, so stiff were his boots. He turned his head back. "And bring shotguns!" he shouted.

All the while, the shrieking and ripping and smashing sounds continued, and if anything, increased in intensity.

Slocum swallowed back the hard knot of terror in his throat and plunged forward into the dark night, pushing his way through what snow had accumulated between the dining cabin and the storage shack. At a distance of what he guessed was halfway to the shed, he paused, his breath feathering into the black sky. He heard a raspy, stuttering sound close by, as if in his own ear, and realized it was his own breathing, coming hard, out of fear.

The sounds continued. The black bulk of the storage shed sat a good fifteen yards away, and the wrecking sounds emanated from within. He couldn't see it clearly enough, but already he had formed an image in his mind of the plank door hanging askew, or ripped from its leather-strap hinges completely, perhaps holes poked in the thick cedar shake roof, the interior a ravaged mess. The beasts, whatever the hell they were—some freakish cross between a grizzly and only the devil knew what else—were probably after food. Maybe the smoked meats hanging from the rafters in the dark shed. Perhaps boxed goods, stored root vegetables, sacks of meal and flour, all ripped and strewn and smashed and scattered.

There was a part of Slocum, though—despite what he had seen, what he had heard, the cold, horrific tingling daggers running up and down his backbone and into his scalp, then straight down into his guts—that doubted this was anything more than a rogue bear.

Or, he thought, pooching his lips at the vaguest of possibilities that this new idea introduced, perhaps this thing was more man than beast? Maybe those two jackasses who attacked him? Might go a long way in explaining why Frenchy acted so odd about them. And why everyone at the Tamarack Logging Camp was so all-fired squirelly and cagey about nearly everything.

Another outburst of growls and howls from the dark and stormy gloom ahead snapped Slocum from his reverie. He raised the lantern high and caught a glimpse of movement, something dark, covered in—what? Fur? Clothes? He could not tell. It looked to have been made from inside a space along the logs, likely the door that had, as he had guessed, been ripped off its hinges.

"Hey!" he shouted, still holding the lantern aloft, still not daring to walk toward sounds that could have been made by a slow cannon blast warring with a bull grizz. And where in the hell were the other men anyway?

He didn't dare turn around, not when there was something—or some *things*—unknown to him somewhere in the dark, not far from him, in fact. He took a step forward, waving the light in an arc before him. He risked one quick peek back over his shoulder and saw the door of the cabin open, a dozen or so loggers huddled together in the doorway, staring out at him.

"Could use some help here!" shouted Slocum in a barking tone. He doubted, though, that they could detect his anger through the howling wind.

Still they didn't do much more than shuffle their feet in place and look at each other. One form broke through them and trudged up the path toward Slocum. It was Ned again, this time carrying a lantern and a shotgun. His pipe was clamped in his mouth.

His grim look mirrored Slocum's. Once he made it to Slocum's side, they walked forward together, slowly advancing on the storage shed. The closer they drew, the farther away the growls and guttural shrieks became. Finally they made it to the door of the shed, or what had but minutes before been a door. Even though the wind had picked up, rousting dervish swirls into their faces, they could see that the wreckage was severe.

The door had been pulled free and lay barely attached to one leather-strap hinge, and Slocum could see some of the roofing—shake shingles—flapping free in the breeze. And when they mustered the strength to look inside, they found bare ropes hanging from the ceiling rafters, ropes that had not long before held shanks of meat cinched tight. Wooden bins of vegetables had been upended, ripped from the walls, and their contents strewn about and stomped on.

"What in the name of all that is holy did this?" shouted Slocum.

Ned didn't reply, merely stared at the wreckage.

"You think it was the skoocoom, or whatever they called it?" Slocum continued, slowly surveying the depressing mess inside the shed, keeping an ear cocked for any sound that might indicate the ransacking beasts might be returning.

"I . . . I don't know what to think. They've come around

plenty at times like earlier, though they only made noise, maybe hurled a piece of firewood against a log wall to get our attention, it seemed, but tonight . . ." Ned turned slowly around the room, holding his lantern aloft. "Tonight they really outdid themselves. If I didn't know it was the blasted skoocoom, I'd swear it was . . ."

Slocum turned on Ned, held his lantern close to the older man's face. "Swear it was what, Ned? You think it was some of the men, don't you? From town? From the Tamarack? Or from somewhere else?"

"I . . . I didn't say anything of the sort. Don't go trying to put words into my mouth, Slocum. You just do the job you were hired to do here and leave such worryings to them who has the right and the authority to worry about such matters." Before Slocum could reply, the man stomped off back to the dining cabin, leaving Slocum alone in the midst of the rubble, wondering what in the hell he'd gotten himself into.

There's one thing none of these men are going to stop me from doing, he thought as he made his way back along the trail. And that's from sleeping in the stable. There are enough horses to keep me warm, and I can protect the Appaloosa should those varmints—whoever or whatever they may be—return. And besides, he thought as he approached the stable, I am damned sure the horses will be easier to get along with, and smell a whole lot better, than a bunkhouse full of men who've been living on beans for weeks.

7

"It wasn't our fault, boss," said the man with the smeared nose. "He just up and attacked us. We went up there like you said, looking for work, and he come at us with an axe. Ain't that right?" He looked at his companion.

The man beside him, thin and equally battered looking, swallowed and nodded, not taking his eyes off the steaming plate of food their boss had before him on his desktop. "Yeah, that's about right."

Torrance Whitaker sighed, continued tucking his napkin under his chin, and lifted his knife and fork. "I did not ask you two men to engage anyone in fisticuffs. In fact, I did not ask you to do a damn thing. My boneheaded son did. But he was acting on what he thought was my behalf, so I will let this episode slide. You were not successful, however, in doing much of anything. Except ticking me off."

"But boss—"

Whitaker thrust his knife at the thicker of the two men. "Don't you call me that. At least not until I get what I want." He thrust a quivering wad of chicken into his mouth.

"What is it you want?"

Whitaker regarded the bold-talking man. "I want Jigger McGee. Everything he owns, in fact. I'd pay a whole lot for that." He smiled, thrust more meat into his maw, chewed. His smile slipped when he saw the two battered men still standing before his desk.

"You two, get the hell out of here. I'm sick of looking at you."

They fidgeted. Whitaker sighed and fingered a coin from his vest pocket, flipped it to the bolder of the two, obviously the brains of the pair. "Go away, clean up, drink, do something. As long as it's away from me."

8

The events of the night before had left Slocum confused, tired, and not a little steamed at the gall of his fellow loggers. Not only had he been acting on their behalf, trying to find out what was ravaging their stock of supplies, but they had the nerve to seem to be accusing him of being in league somehow with whatever or whoever had done the foul deed. True, they hadn't said much to that effect, but the chilly tone was there.

Even Ned, who he'd thought he'd developed a bit of camaraderie with, had been cold toward him this morning. The only one who showed him any amount of gratitude—not that he was looking for it—was Frenchy.

The burly camp cook had chuckled and slopped down a ladleful of gruel, thick as Southern mud, and tossed a handful of raisins and dried apple rings on top. "Good morning, Slocum. You deserve *deux* helpings of raisins today for the help you gave us last night."

"Wasn't enough to prevent the shed from being torn apart."

"True, but keep in mind that it could have been so much worse, *non*?"

Slocum nodded in reluctant agreement, then took his place at one of the tables, the only one that seemed to have a space available for him to sit. He ate in silence, glad, frankly, to be on his own. He brooded for a few minutes while he spooned up the surprisingly tasty hot grains mixed with dried fruit.

He followed the gruel with a couple of cups of hot, black coffee, all the while doing his best not to brood on the thought most looming in his mind—that he should never have ventured this far north for a job. Hell, he shouldn't have come this far north in the winter for anything, not even a woman—though that particular promising approach had worked out for him in the past.

He longed for a normal life, one in which he was no longer a wanted man, on the run from the law. He wanted a life in which he could settle down, perhaps on his own spread somewhere that wasn't too hot in the summer, not too cold in the winter, with grazing and . . . bah! Enough with the self-pity. He knew he had to see this thing through. He was no quitter.

Never had been, and wasn't about to start now. Just because a bunch of burly loggers were too busy grousing about what was happening to them to solve the problem for themselves didn't mean he had to toss in the towel and let them get to him.

No sir, thought Slocum as he stood and carried his bowl, spoon, and cup to the huge copper cauldron beside the stove into which Frenchy was tossing the dirty dishes.

"Frenchy," said Slocum in a voice loud enough for everyone in the place to hear. "I guess it's just about as perfect a day as any to get some work done, don't you think?"

"Sure, sure Slocum," said the cook, looking a bit confused at Slocum's sudden loud utterance.

That was more for me than anyone else, thought Slocum. Got to make sure they don't get to me.

But all these hours later, after they'd gotten to the woodlot they were working, a couple of miles northwest of the main camp, the boss, Jigger's right-hand man, guessed Slocum, who it turned out was Ned, his erstwhile chum from the night before, had brought him quite a distance from the main group.

"I need these six trees limbed out by lunch." He looked at Slocum. "Or no lunch. You got me?"

"Yep," said Slocum. He was happy to play the silly games for as long as he needed to. As long as there was a chit for pay at the end of this deal, he'd do whatever tasks they set him to.

Slocum didn't wait for him to try to explain away whatever it was he wasn't telling Slocum, but instead set right to work. Limbing was a good, if mindless, task for him. He'd done plenty of it in the past and knew enough to get the job done in a decent time frame. Certainly by midday.

"Anything else?"

"That's enough," said Ned, already heading back down the trail that led to the rest of the crew. He offered a half-hearted one-handed wave over his shoulder, a stream of pipe smoke following him back down the trail.

Slocum set to his task. The day was coming off mild, and the sun was a high, bright spot in a clear sky. It was the first fully blue day he'd seen in a week, and the day's warmth filtered down, reaching him in the newly made clearing. Soon he had worked up a full head of steam, chips flying from the gleaming blade of the double-bit axe assigned to him. He'd also been loaned a pair of stout spiked boots to help keep him atop the massive felled trees' rough hides while he swung his axe first left, then right, lopping off endless branches to make the tree into an enormous log.

He wasn't sure how many hours had passed by the time

he stopped for a long, much-needed drink from his canteen. The woods in full sun were still somewhat dark among the massive trunks, but the ghostly mounds and rolling scape of snow reflected the increasing sunlight and gave the quiet forest an odd, yet comforting glow.

For a while at least, he thought. Until dark comes, then this place will probably echo with the shrieks of whatever it is that lurks out here.

And that was when he heard the far-off, but drawing closer, sound of . . . someone singing? And not from the direction of the crew. Who could it be? Another logger working at limbing even farther up the valley than him? He held his hand over his eyes and squinted upslope, using spotting skills he'd employed many times in locating bighorn sheep and mountain goats, deer and wolves far away on hillsides and in terrain similarly riddled with rocks, trees, and blow-downs.

There was a shape, definitely human, moving slowly in his direction. Whoever it was looked to be making a beeline for him, and would reach him in minutes. He had cooled sufficiently that he pulled on his wool button-down shirt back over his tight longhandles. Wouldn't do to catch a lung disorder out in the wilds like this. One cough could lead to a fast trip to Boot Hill.

He lifted down his gun belt hanging where he'd draped it—within reach—close by on a branch nub. He strapped it on and checked his Colt Navy, loosened the leather thong from the hammer, and made sure his long skinning knife was still sheathed. Then he hefted the axe and rested it atop his shoulder and waited.

He didn't have long to wait—whoever it was making his way though the snow wore snowshoes and made good use of them, too, kicking up a fine spray of snow dust, like vanishing feathers, behind him. He was an average-height man, thin, but well clothed for the high country from which he'd descended. On his back Slocum saw what looked to be an ash pack basket. A trapper? This high up? Maybe in the valleys there were plenty of beaver ponds, martens in the forests, maybe weasels, fishers, fox, coyote, wolves, lynx, and bobcat.

He saw a few critter tails bouncing from where they hung from the top of the basket. The man carried a rifle, a Henry from the looks of it, and wore a black-and-red-checked wool coat lined with sheepskin, the thick, full hood worn high, forming a point above his head. Green wool mittens adorned his hands, and black wool trousers flared just above high leather lace-up boots.

Still yards away, the man, his breath pluming out visibly, halted and threw up a hand, but said nothing. Slocum returned the universal signal of greeting.

The trapper resumed his march, slow and steady, through snow that Slocum would have quickly foundered in up to his chest.

When he was but five yards away, the man halted again and pushed the hood back off his head to reveal a round-faced, apple-cheeked woman. She smiled at him, large blue eyes reflecting the sunlight that itself was reflected off the glittering snow all around them. Thick, honeyed hair, the color of fall leaves with sun punching through as they whispered in a breeze, had spilled loose and framed her face, freed from the hood.

"Ho there!"

"Well, ho there, yourself, ma'am," said Slocum, nodding in greeting but still not willing to remove his hand from the butt of his Colt, no matter how lovely the high-country nymph before him might appear.

"What are you doing up here in my woods?" She looked Slocum up and down with an appraising stare, as if thinking about purchasing him for use at a future time. Her slight smirk told him everything he needed to know—she might well be toying with him, though she also probably believed that these woods were her domain, deed or no deed.

Slocum returned the smirk. "Ordinarily, on meeting for the first time, strangers exchange greetings. For instance, I am John. John Slocum. Pleased to meet you—I think. And you are . . . ?" He leaned forward, canting his head as if in expectation of an answer.

Her sudden, wide smile brightened her already welcoming face and told Slocum he had little to fear from her and that she was indeed pulling his leg.

"Serves me right, John Slocum. I'm afraid I've been out here with the critters and such for too long on my own."

"How long has it been?"

"Well, let's put it this way—I see a whole lot of me, but they don't see me. And judging from the ones I've seen, I don't care for that situation to change anytime soon."

"Then why talk to me?"

She appraised him again, looking him up and down, stood hipshot, one mittened hand resting on her cocked hip, one holding the rifle balanced on her opposite thigh. "You . . . I ain't seen before. And you're . . . different somehow."

Slocum kept his eyes on hers while he lowered the axe and sank the blade with a satisfying thunk into the massive butt end of the tree he'd been limbing. "A lesser man might not know how to take that . . . "

"But you are no lesser man, am I right?"

"You are right on that score."

"And you're not lacking in confidence either, am I right?"

"Right again, ma'am. But I still don't know your name."

"Why are you in such an all-fired need to know my name?"

Slocum shrugged. "You seem like someone a lonely logger might want to get to know."

Her smile dropped like a deadfall limb. "I ain't that kind of woman."

"I'm not sure what sort you think I'm referring to, but I can tell you I meant it as a compliment."

Again, she eyed him up and down, let her eyes travel then settle on his face. "I suppose you are sincere. Or at least as much as you think you can be." She chewed her lip, then looked at him as if she'd just come to a decision. She stuck out her hand and stepped forward. "I'm Hella Bridger. Though I think the loggers hereabouts call me something else."

"Pleased to meet you, Hella." They shook hands, and Slocum nodded again to her. "Do I dare ask what the folks hereabouts refer to you as?"

She sighed, then smirked again. "Crazy Trapper Lady."

"And are they correct?"

"In part, I guess. I am a trapper, and I am a lady, in some sense. At least I used to be. And I think crazy is in the eye of the beholder, don't you?"

"Not sure what you mean by that."

"For instance," she said, "I don't necessarily think I'm crazy, but I can understand how other folks, seeing how I live, might think my train's gone around the bend. You know?"

"I think I've been there a few times myself. How do you live? I mean, you're a trapper, I see that."

"Yep, got myself a regular old slice of heaven up here, hundreds, maybe thousands of square miles to roam, to trap, keep my lines moving so I don't overtrap any one area, then I move on, let the critters recover from me taking their loved ones away to the happy critter ground in the sky."

"Why, that's right philosophical of you, ma'am."

She gave him that appraising look again. "Seems like I was right about you, John Slocum."

"How's that?" he said, easing his hand off his revolver's handle as she shouldered her rifle by its leather sling.

"Not many loggers would use a word like 'philosophical' in regular conversation. Or any conversation, for that matter."

"Well, I won't apologize for reading a book now and again."

"Good," she said. "Not enough people in the world who read."

He nodded. "So you know Jigger, then? Or at least his crew—if only by sight."

"I know Jigger McGee. He's a good man, about the only logger worth a spit. He runs his own crews, not like Torrance Whitaker, who hires out everything. The other thing that separates McGee from Whitaker is that Jigger seems to be the only logger to do what I try to do with the critters I trap. He's good to the trees, you know? Doesn't overdo it in any one spot. Now that, I have to admire."

"That's good to know. I'm only on my second day with the outfit. First, if you consider I got a late start yesterday."

There was a lull in the chat, and Slocum pulled in a deep draught of air. "Well, I best get back to it. But it's been a real pleasure to talk with you, Miss Bridger. I hope we can pass the time as pleasantly some other day. I expect, at my current rate, that I'll be here for the duration."

"Fair enough," she said.

They shook hands again, and as she turned to go, Slocum said, "One more thing. I can't believe I'm asking this, but here goes—do you know anything about a creature called the 'skoocoom'?"

"Why?" There was that smirk again. "Do you think you saw it?" But there was something else behind that smirk.

"Yes, in fact. Well, I saw something, fleetingly. I also saw greenish glowing eyes, high up, maybe a couple of feet taller than me. And the sounds we heard were something else."

"And?"

"Isn't that enough?"

"Yes, but what happened at the camp?"

"Why do you ask?"

"Because something is always happening at the Tamarack Logging Camp. It's Jigger's lot in life. At least while he's working to pay off his debt."

So that's it, eh? thought Slocum. Jigger's in debt. "Might help explain why he was in such a hurry to get to town yesterday, but not what happened last night."

She looked at him, eyebrows arched, ready for enlightenment. He obliged. "Something I've never heard or seen evidence of before ripped apart the camp's storehouse, howling and making quite a ruckus. They did things I doubt a man—or a team of them—could have done."

"You said 'they.' You think there was more than one?"

"I do. I didn't get a clear look, but the calls and howls definitely overlapped enough that it was easy to tell there was more than one."

"You might want to check the bunkhouse before you start blaming the poor skoocoom for everything bad that happens at the Tamarack."

"What do you mean by that?"

"Gotta go now, John Slocum!" She saluted him with a mittened hand and swung around in the trail, strode back the way she had come, rifle still slung over her shoulder, long, purposeful strides leading her away from him.

He forgot his concerns over skoocooms and the riled-up, irritated, and thoroughly confusing situation at the Tamarack Logging Camp while he watched Hella Bridger's promising feminine form, swathed as it was in bulky trapper's garb, retreat way back up the mountainside, cutting long strides in the deep snow without rest, traversing the switchbacks and gaining high ground.

As he watched her move gracefully up the slope, he wondered what she meant by that last remark—the one she'd not bothered to explain. It sounded to him as if she knew something about some of the men in the bunkhouse, maybe that they were up to something no good. That would verify what he suspected. That while the skoocoom might or might not exist, there sure as hell were bad elements in the bunkhouse, men who might be working to sabotage Jigger's operation from within. But why was everyone so closemouthed about it all?

As if she knew he'd still be watching her, just before she disappeared from sight by elevation, she turned and waved—a big, wide-armed wave. He smiled and waved back. What a mysterious woman, he thought. She spoke alternately like a mountain woman and like someone well educated.

Hefting the axe, Slocum turned back to the next tree that needed limbing. And why shouldn't he find a curious creature like that up here in Oregon's Cascades? It was not like this trip hadn't yielded any number of odd characters and situations, and perhaps even creatures, so far. He hoped he'd run into her again. She was one curiosity he'd like to see more of.

9

In his office at the rear of the Bluebird Saloon, Dance Hall, and Eatery, the nexus of what he liked to think of as his expanding business empire, Torrance Whitaker leaned back in his desk chair, his ample girth testing the durability of the thick spring mechanism allowing it to rock. Problem was, when he kicked all the way back, his legs dangled, and unless he was close enough to the desk's edge to grasp it with a pudgy hand, Torrance found the chair too unpredict-able, not at all trustworthy, and the damnable thing would upend him, ass over teakettle. The last time, he'd gotten wedged somehow between the wall, the chair, and the desk. He'd had to yelp for his boy, Jordan, the young fool who worked for him—and also happened to be his long-lost son—to come and free him from the embarrassing spot.

But he did so like to lean back, waggle in the chair a bit, suck on a cigar, and plan his next moves. And that was exactly what he found himself doing on that evening, min-utes after he'd left the throng in the street, wondering if he'd won the volley of threats and insults he'd exchanged with that cursed Jigger McGee, or if the foul little lumberman had gotten the upper hand.

Whitaker finally shrugged, nudged the chair into a weak rocking motion, and plumed blue smoke toward the hazy ceiling. In the end, he would win, as he always did. Because brains and money would win the day, not anger and brute force. And those last two were the things Jigger possessed. At least that was what Whitaker chose to believe. At least for the night—he didn't have the strength to begin second-guessing himself.

No matter. He had no intention of allowing McGee to sell his logs to anyone for a profit. Oh, the wood was desirable all right, but Whitaker wanted it all for himself. And preferably without paying for it. If he could just prevent Jigger McGee from keeping up with his lease payments on that tree-studded mountain valley.

"Papa?"

Curse that little man anyway. If he thought Torrance Whitaker was going to let a little thing like one man's livelihood stand in the way of his putting a lock on the entire region's rich resources—wood, water, and minerals—he'd better do some hard thinking.

"Hey, Papa?"

"Huh?" Whitaker spun around—or attempted to. The chair squawked and bobbed, but stayed tipped back. Whitaker could barely see over his left shoulder toward the cracked door. "What? Who is it? Jordan, that you?"

"Yeah, Papa. I was wonderin'—"

"Yeah, yeah—your wondering doesn't concern me at present. What does, however, is the fact that those two morons you suggested to send to work for Jigger up at the Tamarack apparently haven't yet succeeded in putting an end to that little fool's operations."

"Hey now, Papa, they're my friends."

"And that is precisely why nothing useful has happened.

And for that, I blame your mother, God rest her. She had fine points, to be sure, but she unfortunately saddled your brain with a lot to be desired." All the while Whitaker spoke, he pumped his legs as if he were urging a horse to gallop faster. It didn't seem to help. In fact, the chair wagged and bucked and spun him ever closer toward the back wall.

"You want help, Papa?" Jordan moved into the room, but his boss held up an arm.

"No! I certainly don't need your assistance to sit in my chair. That is a task I can do alone, thank you very much. What I do need is someone or something more effective up at the Tamarack! Since I'm stuck with you, get the hell out of here and figure out a plan to infiltrate that foul camp and bring it to its knees. I want to make McGee scream in agony. I want him to beg me to take his business from him."

"But Papa, Jigger McGee isn't a bad man. He's a hard-working man with a whole lot of people depending on him for their week's wages. He's a businessman, just like you." The big, thick-featured young man stared at his father with a mix of pity and blank numbness.

Whitaker's cigar drooped in his mouth, and he returned the stare. "What in the name of all that is holy did I saddle myself with, taking you on after your mother, God rest her, up and died while I was incarcerated?"

"But I'm your boy, your own son, Papa."

"More's the pity. And now you've gone and gotten not only softheaded on me about that dolt Jigger, but you've fallen for his scrappy little daughter. A more ornery creature you'll not find."

"Papa, don't say that about Ermaline. She's my sweetheart and you yourself gave us your blessing, isn't that right?"

Torrance chewed the cigar and nodded slowly, a smile working its way back onto his face. Yes, I did, he thought.

And while I merely guessed before how I might work this foolish dalliance to my advantage, now I know exactly how I'm going to do that.

"Now I would like you to do me a favor, Jordan."

The boy leaned toward his father. "Yes, Papa? Anything."

"I'd like for you to leave me alone for a while. I have important thinking to do. But so do you."

"Oh, okay, Papa. Call me if you need me." With that the big boy left, clunking the door too hard once again, as Whitaker always told him not to.

What I need, thought Torrance Whitaker to himself, is someone who will remove this headache from me so I can concentrate my copious mental abilities on larger, more pressing concerns—such as preparing for the imminent arrival of the mining consortium's representatives. As soon as I can convince them I have something to offer them, that is . . .

If he could impress them, convince them that they were about to invest in a property worth, well, worth its weight— and then some—in gold, perhaps they would cement the deal with a cash deposit, a payment that would put Whitaker right where he wanted to be, had longed to be for so much of his life. Rubbing elbows with the richest of the rich.

He envied the Silver Barons, the Copper Kings, the Gold Gods. And he had vowed years ago to become one of them, by hook or by crook. Unfortunately it had been a long, rocky road from there to here. Many years had passed and many more business dealings, but none of them, for one reason or another, had gotten him as close to fulfilling his dream as this one.

When he'd arrived in the timber-rich valley, only two years before, there was something about it—a raw, vast wild place that had the look of being pregnant with promise. He knew there was something extra special about it, something that set his inner bells pealing with a fervor he'd not felt since his first youthful days as a gold claims speculator. That was his fancy way of justifying his all-but-outright theft of nearly played-out claims from equally played-out prospectors.

The old rock hounds had been all too eager to sell for pennies on the dollar and he had turned around and sold each to fresh rubes from back East. But at a substantial profit. By the time the new arrivals realized they'd been had, he was miles away, repeating the simple but effective process.

And that had led him to larger and larger ventures, which had nearly gotten him what he'd wanted—a fortune—but then someone he'd had dealings with years before had come around again, recognized him, and that, as they say, had been that. He'd been hauled off to spend four years making big rocks into smaller rocks out in a hellish place in the desert.

So when he got out, he vowed never again to sweat, and certainly not to do it while working. No sir, he'd head north, toward some place that offered snow in the winters, and temperatures in the summers that were at least cool and shady enough that he might duck out of the sunlight when the hottest months came. And that was how he came to find Timber Hills—so named by that damnable Jigger.

As he'd hoped, the place had offered all he wanted and more, in addition to a plethora of business opportunities that the locals—sheep all—had not yet (nor would they ever, if left to their own devices) recognized. But he, Torrance Whitaker, had. And now here he was, a scant two years later, poised to become the richest man in all the Northwest region, a Territorial Titan!

Whitaker chuckled, then the chuckle unspooled into a full-blown laugh, a belly shaker that rocked the chair . . . too hard. Too late he felt the wheeled feet slip, scoot forward, then back he went, slamming his head into the plank wall before flopping onto his back on the cold plank floor, his cigar and arms and legs crabbing and wagging upward as if he were an overturned turtle. Still, he chuckled at how very well, despite a few logs across the road, his life was turning out.

10

"Say, Ned." Slocum shifted the axe on his shoulder.

"Mm?" said the pipe-smoking man as they trudged side by side down the long slope to the sledge road that could take them back to the Tamarack Camp.

"Have you had any dealings with a, well, a trapper who's a woman?" Slocum asked.

The man's face broke into a smile for the first time since Slocum had met him the day before. Without breaking stride, he said, "So you've met the Crazy Trapper Lady, eh?"

"She said that's what people call her. I didn't think she was all that crazy myself."

Ned came to a sudden halt, faced Slocum. "You spoke with her?"

A couple of the other men who'd been within earshot also stopped and stepped close.

"Sure I did," said Slocum. "I didn't have much choice. She came right up to me."

"Huh," said one of the other men. "You mean to say she can talk?"

"Of course she can talk. And walk, and laugh, and carry a rifle like she knows what she can do with it, too."

Ned chuckled, shaking his head. "I haven't known you for long, Slocum, but I'd say that it doesn't surprise me that of all the men from the Tamarack who've seen her, you'd be the one she approaches. Now why is that, you reckon?"

It was Slocum's turn to smile. "If I had to guess, I'd say it's the big gun I carry."

"Oh boy, will you listen to this fella?" Ned shook his head. "All I know or care about, Slocum, is that you're the best limber I've had on the crew in many a moon. So you might get a chance to see your crazy lady again tomorrow."

"Oh?" said Slocum, eyebrows raised. "I'm not sure I like where this conversation is headed."

"Like it or not, I'm the foreman, least until Jigger gets back, so you'll just have to put up with it."

"You got it," said Slocum. "Might I ask what Jigger's story is?"

"Story?" said Ned.

"Yeah, you know. How'd he come to own this mountain valley, and this logging outfit, anyway?"

"Oh, he doesn't own the mountain, at least not anymore. He just leases the timber rights. And that's what galls Whitaker the most, I'd guess." Ned drew on his pipe, frowned when he found it had gone out.

"Whitaker?" Hella mentioned that name, too, thought Slocum.

"Yep, a newcomer of sorts, much like yourself, but he's been around these parts for a couple of years now. Fancies himself a big money man, but all he's done so far around here is win the Bluebird Saloon in a card game, then poke his sniffer into everybody's business. I reckon it's been effective, as he's gotten a whole lot of folks beholden to him for money and favors and whatnot. Fool and his money are soon parted, or something like that." Ned puffed hard on the pipe and sent fragrant smoke twisting upward.

"Even Jigger?" said Slocum.

Ned regarded him, then nodded slowly. "Yeah, I guess you could say so. You see, Jigger has a child, his only one, a girl name of Ermaline. Well, you know how tough Jigger is?"

Slocum nodded, only guessing at the man's level of toughness, but not wanting to slow the story once he'd finally gotten Ned, or anyone for that matter, to talk with him about Jigger.

"Well, sir, Ermaline used to be part of the crew up here at the Tamarack. Her mama died years back and Jigger just kept right on logging, taking that girl all over the mountains in these parts. She grew up salty, tough as a boot, and not inclined to take anything untoward from anyone."

He drew on the pipe, then continued. "But a stranger come in one day when the girl was still a young thing in most ways, except for how she looked. You see, Ermaline had begun filling out her longhandles in a few different directions than most loggers do. Well, Jigger caught this randy young log hand cornering Ermaline in the cook shack. He needn't have worried, though. Ermaline is part wolverine, part bobcat, and all devil. She about clawed that young man's eyes out and his head off. He limped on out of here aching all over once she and Jigger got through with him."

"Where's this Ermaline at now?"

"That's where the story gets interesting." Ned pulled the pipe from his mouth. "Now, you'll stop me if this gets too boring for you, won't you?" He winked. "Shortly after the incident with the young logger, Jigger shunted Ermaline off to live with her aunt, Jigger's dead wife's sister, back in Saint Louis. But that didn't go over too well with the girl, who ran off at once. They found her again, and eventually, after what

I imagine was a whole lot of hard work, she settled down and even took to wearing dresses. Now that she's graduated from what they call a 'finishing school,' she come back to Timber Hills to see her pappy."

"Why do I feel that something odd happened, that the story's about to take a turn that no one wanted?"

Ned touched a finger to the side of his nose and nodded. "That's because something like that did happen. Wasn't but a couple of days after she got here she met a man."

"And not just any man, I'll bet," said Slocum.

"No sir, you got that right. It's a double smack to the chops the way Jigger sees it. And rightly so, for the man she became smitten with is none other than Torrance Whitaker's own son, Jordan. My word, but he's as dumb as he is big. I'll say this for the lad, though—he doesn't seem to have a single bone in his body that's half as mean as his father. But that don't mean a thing to Jigger. Oh, it's a rum mess, it is, it is."

They walked on in silence a few strides, then Slocum spoke.

"Why did Jigger end up selling this plentiful valley when he could have held on to it and made a fortune later?"

"He needed to pay for his daughter's fancy schooling. He got scared and took the first offer that come along."

"Let me guess—from this Torrance Whitaker fellow."

"The very one. Jigger at least had the presence of mind to keep the logging rights as a lease. But only if he keeps up with his lease payments on it to the bank."

"And he has?"

"It's been hairy, and he's been late a few times, but this crew's dedicated to him. He's a surly little man, and you don't want to get on the wrong side of him, but once you've proved yourself to Jigger, he'll fight to the death for you."

"I got that impression from him, even in the short amount of time I met him on the trail."

"Yep, he was headed off to the broker's spread down-country to negotiate on the last few loads of logs, as well as the ones we're working on now. And hopefully he got paid for them. Then he was going to head to town, make it to the bank, buy supplies. And head back."

"He had to see his daughter, too, I suppose."

Ned nodded. "Yep, if they're speaking again. Jigger loves her with a fierceness that's unstoppable, but that girl did the ultimate in betrayal when she took up with that dimwitted spawn of Torrance Whitaker. In her defense, she had no idea what sort of man Whitaker was when she come back to these parts. He'd sneaked in well after she left."

"The man at the bar in town, he told me that there's a renewed market for logs. A demand from the Orient."

"Yep, that's been a lifesaver. Oh, there's always need of good, quality logs from these hills, but the prices those boys are paying are far beyond anything we've been paid for our logs in the past. Jigger's doing his best to keep his old friend, Deke Tiffins, the log broker, supplied. He's been a true friend to Jigger, but rumor has it he's been feeling the squeeze by Whitaker, too."

He shook his head. "Don't know what the weasel has on him, but that can only mean bad things for Jigger. So that's why we're working as fast and hard as we can to fell these trees and make logs. That's why Jigger's put the word out that he's hiring, even though he really doesn't have the money to go out paying for a whole lot of new men."

Worry must have flashed across Slocum's face, because Ned smiled. "Don't you worry. Ol' Jigger never backed off on a promise, nor ever not paid a man, nor for that matter, he never ever let a man go hungry on Tamarack time."

"Good to know," said Slocum. And as he walked along the rest of the trip down the valley in silence, he wondered more and more about the skoocoom and about the Crazy

Trapper Lady, aka Hella Bridger, and less and less about Jigger McGee and his money woes. He'd heard such stories before.

In Slocum's experience, good intentions such as Jigger's eventually led to situations people never expected. He hoped they were good ones.

11

Jigger's spirits rose with each step until his brief, sour-tasting encounter with Torrance Whitaker dissipated. By the time he reached the steps of the bank, he was nearly back to feeling his excitement about getting paid for his logs. But not quite all the way. And it was only because Whitaker had to get that dig in about his own dear Ermaline being betrothed to Jordan, that dimwitted offspring of Whitaker.

"How could she?" he said aloud as his gnarled work-hardened hand closed on the brass door handle of the bank's front door. It opened wide, with no answer to his question, but with a low squawk and a loud, brassy bell's ring that indicated he was about to conduct business.

"To what do I owe the pleasure, Mr. McGee?" said Burke, the banker. "I thought this little meeting of ours was surely due to be postponed."

"And why did you think that might happen, eh, Burke?" Jigger hoisted his big leather satchel onto the counter with a thud. "As it happens, I have my payment right here."

The banker's confident smile drooped. "Well . . . ah, good. That's good. Yessiree."

Jigger stood by smiling, eyes narrowed a bit. Finally he said, "How's that feel, eh? Ha! It's good to watch you squirm, Burke. I been the one pinned by your gaze for far too long. I'm enjoying this, sure as shootin', I'm enjoying myself."

Jigger rubbed his hands together, then said, "All right, enough of old home week. I got things to do and people to see. Ain't often a loggin' man gets into town. Let's get this all counted up nice and fair and square, and I can get goin' about my business."

Jigger watched the banker's eyes widen as he took out the money, set it on the counter, in nice, even stacks. "Now, you count and I'll count, and we'll either agree or go back and count it all over again. And I know neither of us wants to be in here late, especially as it's a fine cold evening and there's lots to do. And lest I forget, I'm going to need a signed receipt for all that money, Burke."

"Why, of course you'll get one. Same as all my customers." The man tried to look as if he'd been slapped, but it was a weak attempt, Jigger knew.

"I wasn't so sure, now that you're lorded over by his holiness, Torrance Whitaker."

"Whatever do you mean?" said Burke, pausing in mid-count.

"Oh, don't give me that hill of beans, Burke! You know as well as me that Whitaker bought his way onto the board. Heck, unless he's lying to me—which now that I think on it is entirely possible—he's the new ramrod of this bankin' outfit. Shameless, I tell you. I never in all my days seen a town as scrimy and whiny and shameless. Used to be we all had a backbone. But since that tub of bear grease rolled on into our midst, why, we've been nothing but backside-kissing fools!" Jigger pounded a fist hand on the counter. A stack of coins shook and slid to the side.

"Please, Mr. McGee," said the red-faced banker. "I'm trying to keep a straight tally."

"And see that you do . . . " Jigger was in high dudgeon, could feel the familiar sensation. Why, since he had to spend the night in Timber Hills, he might just make a quick tour of the various establishments, make sure these people knew exactly what they were doing in groveling to ol' Whitaker, that sidewinding rascal.

Start out at the Plug Nickel, head on down to Rollo's House of Sport, then end the tour with a visit to Whitaker's own dump, the Bluebird. Maybe by then he'd have thought of something to say to the fat man.

It didn't take Burke long to come to a figure that they both agreed was the correct amount of the cash from Jigger's satchel. He made out a formal receipt, signed it before Jigger, pointed a tapping finger to where he wanted Jigger to countersign, then folded it in thirds, sealed it with a glob of hot wax, which impressed Jigger somewhat, and slid the paper across the counter to McGee.

"Thank you kindly, Burke. Pleasure doing business with you." Jigger doffed his wool stocking cap, stuffed the letter into his satchel, and headed on out the door and back into the bitter cold evening. He pulled in a deep lungful of air, still wearing his smile—for he knew where he was headed and what he was going to get up to. Stir up some coals under the asses of these cushy-bottomed town dwellers! But first he had to tend to family matters. Had to see if Ermaline was in—where else would she be? Sparking with that useless lunk, Jordan Whitaker?

"Oh, what is she thinking?" he muttered again, crossing the street to Mrs. Tigg's boardinghouse. He stood before the front door, dim lamp glow from inside the sitting room barely lighting the entry. He gave himself a once-over look-see, banged his knee-high leather boots together at the heel, readjusted his knitted hat, smoothing it and pulling its ribbed rim down to just above his bushy eyebrows. He ran a knobby hand down his mustache and beard, smoothing them, combing lightly with his fingers to make sure there wasn't any leftover jerky or piecrust stuck in there, then cleared his throat and rapped hard on the white-painted door with his big knuckles.

Within moments he heard footsteps—boot heels, fast, quick, sure, had to be a woman's—on the floor inside, drawing closer. He cleared his throat again and pulled a wide smile. The door handle turned, the door swung inward, and there was his little girl, Ermaline, looking so pretty.

It had been two weeks since he'd seen her, and she looked as lovely as he ever remembered her looking—from when she was a swaddled bairn in her mother's arms through her little girly years, and later, when it was just the two of them—and now here she was, a lovely, grown-up woman. And wearing a pretty dress and all. She even had long hair. She'd been back for some months, but he still couldn't quite get over the changes in his little girl.

"Daddy!"

12

Their hug lasted longer than Jigger would have liked, given as they were still on the doorstep of the boardinghouse. He didn't mind that his daughter liked to hug, always had been a hugger, for that matter. He always liked it, made him feel like he was special, but in the public eye, it made him feel weak, queasy. Even if it was his own daughter. But he also knew this wouldn't last, this happy feeling. Because as much as he wanted to spend time with his daughter—and he didn't care what it was they did, share a pot of tea, maybe some buttered biscuits, take a walk in the cold night air—he had to get to the point of his stopping to see her.

"Ermaline, my girly," said Jigger.

She smiled and led him into the front sitting room of the boardinghouse. No one else was in the room, and a small fire crackled in the woodstove in the center of the south wall.

"I was reading when you knocked."

"Sorry 'bout that," said Jigger, turning the rolled cuff of his knitted hat in his gnarled hands. It felt right odd, being inside a real building, especially a fancy house in town. But she seemed to like it and that was what mattered. Though maybe she'd gotten too much of a taste for town and the suspicious ways of its dwellers.

"Don't be silly, Daddy. I'd rather visit with you anytime than read some old book."

"I thought you liked readin' them things."

"I do, but I like spending time with you even more."

"Hmm," he said, rubbing his chin. "I do like the sound of that. But how about town living? That suit you more than being out at the Tamarack?"

Ermaline dropped into a stuffed chair with a sigh. "Oh, Daddy. That's not a fair question." She looked at him. "Since I got back to Timber Hills, my life has gotten more . . . complicated. Otherwise I'd be out at the camp right now. You know that." She smiled.

"Do I?" He knew it was a low blow, but he had to get to the truth. Here goes, he said to himself.

"What do you mean, Daddy?"

There was a hint of suspicion in her voice, and justifiably so, he thought with a sliver of pride. After all, he'd raised her to be savvy with folks, to get to know what they were really talking about. The words behind their words, so to speak. That skill had rarely let him down.

"What I mean, daughter, is, well . . . " Dang it! Why couldn't he just get to the point where she was concerned? He didn't have a problem telling his men just where the bear went when he had to, so why was his little girl any different?

"Out with it, Daddy!" She stamped her feet just like her mother used to do.

"Okay then. It seems to me you are bound and determined to roust me at every turn."

"What do you mean?"

"That Whitaker boy. He's, why, he's nothing but a . . .

lump! Just like his father, only near as I can tell, he ain't fit to make a patch on the old shyster's ass. And I don't give backhanded comments easily, especially to the likes of that weasel, Whitaker."

Then he saw another look that reminded him of his long-dead wife and mother of this child—she had that jaw set firm, and sparks nearly shot right out of her eyes at him. But she said nothing—yet. He knew it was coming. So he took his chance while he could.

"I've been told that you intend to marry up with that . . . great lump of a boy. Is that the case?"

Her fists were balled now, and though he knew she wasn't about to lay a hand on him, he wasn't quite sure just what she intended to do.

"I don't know where you heard that, Daddy." Her voice was measured, and she spoke through clenched teeth. "But I will tell you that maybe I just will. Nothing of the sort has been said, but you would have been the first person to know—at least from me!"

Jigger smiled and slapped his knee. "I knew it! I knew that sack of dung was lying to me. Right to my face! I should have expected no less!"

Then his daughter did a curious thing. She narrowed her eyes and, in an even tone, said, "Maybe Mr. Whitaker is right, Daddy. Maybe it's time for a change of guard in Timber Hills."

"What are you saying, daughter? What's that evil man done to your thinking?"

"He hasn't done anything. But it seems to me he's not all that wrong. He said that since I know a thing or two about logging, and since I also went to school back East, he's asked me to help him manage his business dealings."

"What?" Jigger's own fists clenched and unclenched, like two callused hearts beating out of control.

"You heard me," she said with a smirk. "He also said that maybe you should step aside, let others come in and set up shop here in Timber Hills. Fresh blood."

"Step aside? Step aside?" Jigger whirled about the small, fancy room, waving his arms as if he were trying to take flight. "Why, you know that this town wouldn't even be here if it weren't for me and my two dead partners, rest their souls! I employed every person in this town at one time or another. Logging is the lifeblood of this town, hang it all!"

"But times are changing, Daddy. There's more to life than chopping down trees!"

Jigger felt as if he'd been punched straight in the gut. The air left him in a whoosh. What could he do? This was no daughter he knew. "Can't believe you just said that to me, girly. I . . . I don't know you anymore." He turned his back to her and reeled from the room, and she just watched him go. They each knew the other was as stubborn as a kicking mule and would never consider giving in to the other. So she let him go.

Once he was outside, the cold air helped sharpen Jigger's senses. It stung going in, pinched his nose, and burned his cheeks. It felt good, and reminded him of why he had come to town. This situation with his daughter was not good, not good at all. But surely the girl would come to her senses.

He had to think of a way to make that happen even faster—just needed time, time to think, time to come up with a plan to run Whitaker and his dumb boy out of town once and for all, before they did anything more to foul his dear Ermaline's mind. He just didn't understand it; she'd always been an independent sort, able to see through the fancy trickeries of magic makers. Bu not this time.

He shook his head. Save it for the trail, Jigger—you got a whole camp of men back in the mountains waiting on you, he told himself. He made straight for Bumpy's General

Store, knowing that while the man would have closed up for the night, he'd fill Jigger's order, have it ready to go on the back loading dock by first light.

And then he'd have himself a drink or three, see if the whole town felt as his daughter did. Might be he'd wind the night up at the Bluebird, find out what Whitaker had to offer.

13

Slocum awoke early the next morning with a single thought compelling him to get up and out before the rest of the early-rising camp stretched and yawned. Something had gnawed at him all night, even as he'd had a surprisingly peaceful sleep.

The night spent in the stable, tight though it was, was also vastly more comfortable and restful than spending time in the bunkhouse with all its stinks and groans and snores. Horses brought their own such potential interruptions to sleep, but he'd always preferred the company of animals to people, and for that he was grateful.

He'd awakened with a single mission on his mind—come hell or high water, he was determined to get to the bottom of this skoocoom business. In all his days roving the trails of the West, he'd come across a number of things that were either outright lies, slowly explained away as hoaxes, or genuine mysteries. He suspected this would fall somewhere in the middle, though even he had doubts as to its status as inexplicable. He certainly couldn't explain it away—yet.

As he tugged on his second boot, he vowed, too, to find the source of his suspicion regarding those two men who'd attacked him. They'd scampered off before he'd returned. At least he had roughed them up good, enough so that they would be sporting evidence of their lost battle for some time to come. Now all he had to do was track them, or whoever had ripped apart the storehouse. Were those two men pretending to be skoocooms? He hoped to find out once he hit the woods and looked for sign—no easy task considering all the foul weather they'd had.

As he high-stepped along the drifted-in path to the savaged storehouse, Slocum bent low, the just-rising sun offering enough reflected glow to assist him in his search for clues. But it was a fruitless search, as he suspected it might well be, given the weather's turn.

Still, if the loggers wouldn't take the opportunity to follow the filled-in dimples of the tracks that led away to the edge of the close-by forest and beyond, into the still-dark trees, then he would.

"Wish I wasn't so curious," he said in a mumble, as a stiff breeze kicked up and slapped him in the face. He flipped up the tall sheepskin collar of his mackinaw and cradled his rifle in the crook of one arm. In the other he hoisted the Colt Navy free of the holster, thoughts of the unearthly shrieks and howls of the other night dogging him. He pulled in a deep breath and headed on in.

Once he found himself well into the tree line, the stiff wind became nothing more than a high-up soughing in the treetops. Down at ground level there was barely a breeze. And as he'd hoped, the well-trammeled path had barely been dusted in. He bent low and peered down into the snowy tracks, cursing himself for not bringing a lamp. The daylight slowly filtered in through the trunks of the trees, but it would be chasing him the deeper he ventured into the forest.

He didn't have all that much time to pursue this path, as he had to get back for breakfast—something he sorely wanted—or he'd go without until lunchtime. And the prospect of limbing trees on an empty stomach was not a possibility. He didn't think he could withstand that for too many swings of the axe.

He squinted into a couple of the deep prints, tugged the end of a leather glove off with his teeth, then felt down in there. Despite the numbing cold, his fingertips felt a series of deep founded depressions where a man's boot toe would be, *should* be. But the print was much wider at the toe than at the other end. The rest of the track also bore little resemblance to a man's boot print. And overall, it was much, much larger—both in length and width—than any print he'd seen made by a man. It was not unlike a grizzly track, but he'd never seen anything that big, and he'd seen a few big ol' bull grizzlies in his day. Even tangled with a few, and counted himself far too lucky to have lived.

What would happen if he tangled with whatever the hell this thing was? What if it was something more than a couple of pissed-off loggers plotting out some odd revenge on Jigger McGee?

And the kicker of this entire set of tracks he was following was that it was made, as near as he could tell, by two creatures. He paused, crouched in the snow, in the quiet, dim forest, looking around at the slowly lightening landscape. And that was when the creeping, hair-raising feeling once again overtook him, draped itself over him like an invisible cloak of tremors and icy fingertips.

Something was watching him. And whatever it was, it wasn't very far away. All of a sudden, the idea of tracking and following this cold trail didn't seem like a very good one. Not at all. He couldn't put a finger on it, but he knew, just as he knew that if he stopped breathing he'd die, that he had to get out of there and back to the camp. Something in this forest was watching him—had probably been watching him since he'd walked in there—and really didn't want him there.

The feeling clung to him well past the edge of the trees and back into the camp clearing.

14

Even before he opened an eye, Jigger knew why he would get a later start than he wanted, hitting the trail away from Timber Hills and back toward his mountains and the Tamarack Camp. He'd overindulged at the bars. Hell, after the first two he didn't know where he'd ended up.

"Oh . . ." he mumbled as he dimly recalled his thoughts from earlier in the evening of stopping off at the Bluebird to give Whitaker a piece of his mind. It seemed like he hadn't ever gotten there, though he couldn't say that with full confidence. All he could recall was that people he knew—and that was just about everyone in town—insisted on buying him drinks. That was grand, until now.

He groaned again. How many had he had? Snake juice never trailed fond memories behind, much as he and every other person who'd ever overindulged in it sought to prove otherwise. He sat up in the stable—yes, that was where he ended up, thank God. By his boys—he could sense them before he saw them. They must have done the same, and knew he was waking, for they nickered in the dim light of the barn.

What time it was, he had no idea, but judging from the sunlight slanting through the gaps in the boards, it was near midmorning. Half the day wasted! No wonder his bladder pounded with each strained thud of his heart, like a cranky grizz cub stuck in his gut, trying to punch its way out. He slowly pushed to his feet and, scrabbling with shaking hands, felt for the side of the stall, found the puckered boards, cribbed slick by countless bored horses, and slowly dragged himself to his feet. Relieved to feel he still wore his boots, Jigger took a hesitant, faltering step forward, then another. Good, he was on his way.

He ambled slowly, if not entirely steadily, to the back door of the place, past ol' Amos, proprietor of the livery, who wisely kept his comments private, and relieved himself on a steaming mound of dung-soiled straw. As he made his way back inside, wincing from the piercing sunlight, he said to Amos, "Whatever I done, just tally it up. I'm good for it."

"Only thing you done is followed the recipe for a large-size hangover. And that's one thing ain't nobody can help you pay for!" That time he didn't keep any comment to himself. He let loose with a laugh, slapped his knee, and shook his head as he tucked into a stall that required his services.

"Funny man, Amos. You're a funny man. Ha."

It took Jigger another hour to collect his gear and his wits, and to drink a potful of hot coffee spiked with Amos's own approved solution—liberal splashes of red-eye. By the time he'd finished his third such cup, Jigger was feeling downright alive, and he never had to help hitch the boys. Amos had it done. Then the liveryman helped him hoist up into the sledge and pointed him in the direction of the mercantile.

"Bump says he has all your goods ready and waiting. Even has a boy to load it up so's you don't have to climb down."

"Seems like everyone's catering to my every whim today," said Jigger.

"Well." Amos smiled. "We all figure it's the least we can do. After all, it ain't every night we all get treated to a rendition of something you called 'The Rime of the Ancient Mariner'—and especially not by a half-dressed logger—now is it?"

He smacked the nearest Belgian on the flank and laughed, watching Jigger's eyes widen and jaw drop as they slid away toward the store.

Jigger experienced more of the same, but not much more of the story of how he'd spent the previous night. He had been assured he'd not broken anything other than some sort of unwritten laws concerning singing and the human ear. Soon the sledge was loaded, strapped down tight, and as he was ready to slap lines, ol' Bumpy handed up a back-pocket bottle of whiskey.

"Keep the edge off and the skoocooms from gettin' too close on your ride back up into the hills!"

"I thank you kindly, Bump. 'Til next time!"

"Thanks for the warning!"

From high in the northward hills overlooking the little smoky town of Timber Hills, two men stood just inside a thick stand of trees. The larger of the two, wearing a crude and bloodied bandage wrapped across his swollen face, lowered a brass spyglass and handed it to the smaller man.

They melted back into the shadows of the trees as Jigger McGee's loaded sledge, towed by a brawny two-horse team, made its slow, steady way out the west end of the little town's main street, then angled north toward the foothills that led to the mountains.

15

Well into his day limbing freshly felled giant pine trees, Slocum had shucked his heavy wool coat and was considering doing the same for his heavy button-down shirt, when a shout stayed his axe's rising swing.

"Ho there! Slocum!" Ned shouted from a standing position on a sledge pulled by two stout black horses he remembered from the stable back at camp.

Slocum paused, grateful for the rest. "What can I do for you, Ned?"

The man pulled his pipe from its customary spot clamped between his lips. "I tell you, Slocum. Me and the boys are getting mighty jittery."

"About what?"

"Balzac and Titus just came back to camp."

"Who are they?"

"If you met 'em, you'd never forget 'em. They're Jigger's pride and joy, his team of Belgians. We have other teams, but he babies those two something fierce. And we heard tell there's a storm coming. Fixing to be a real whopper. Make that one we had just before you got here to look like kitten's work."

"Has anybody set out to find Jigger?" said Slocum. "Might be he's holed up wounded alongside the road somewhere between here and town."

"Yeah, yeah, I sent out Donny and Bert, but they came up short—empty-handed, so to speak."

Slocum slammed his axe head into place. The blatant worry on Ned's otherwise mellow face was undeniable. "I imagine you need someone with trail experience who can take a look-see, find out where in the heck ol' Jigger might be."

"That's the long and short of it, yep. We need someone who can find his way in and out of these woods on snowshoe. If the storm shapes up to be half as bad as ol' Fincherson's game leg is telling him—and it's never wrong—this one's going to be a doozy. If Jigger's hurt and stoved-up somewhere along the trail, we need to get to him before it hits."

"I'll gladly do all I can to help find Jigger, but Ned, if you need someone with snowshoe experience and who knows these woods, why are you sending me out? I'm the newest one here. And I have more saddle experience than snowshoe time."

The man let out a snort of laughter. "Don't let it bother you. You'll be helping me. We're going out together. Frenchy will be in charge of the boys. I've sent half of them back to camp to lay in more firewood, sent a few boys out to scare up some meat, and Frenchy's cooking up a storm. Those skoocooms all but cleaned us out of food stores. And now that Jigger's team come back only half-filled, as if someone had cherry-picked through it—we need all the food we can get."

"Especially if there's a storm coming."

"Yep."

Slocum was only too glad to get a respite from his work. He enjoyed the steady, mindless labor of lopping off branches, big and small, but after a few hours, it truly was numbing. His arms ached and he suspected, despite the full days the men seemed to be putting in, that he was working twice as hard as everyone else. Well, no, he knew that wasn't really the case, but he couldn't help thinking it. He also was about ready to eat a whole side of beef himself.

As if the mere thought of the word "skoocoom" was enough to conjure up sounds from the beasts, roars and howls erupted from the dark woods on each side of the trail. Ned and Slocum exchanged raised-eyebrow looks, then Slocum gathered his gear and climbed onto the sledge.

With his pipe clamped fiercely between his teeth, Ned whipped the two-horse team into a mane-flying frenzy. But it didn't seem enough to outdistance them from the source of the sounds. Nor did it outrun the rocks and chunks of snow-crusted branches that rained down on them from either side.

It had been more than a day since anyone at the camp had heard from or seen signs of the creatures, but now it seemed they were making a comeback—and from the sounds of it, they were lining both sides of the trail.

Only after a few hundred yards did the sledge begin to outdistance the eerie sounds. By the time the men reached the camp, the howls had become nothing but a ringing memory. And one more thing that made Slocum wonder just what he'd gotten himself into.

16

"It's shaping up to be a real a corker, make no mistake, Slocum. One thing we got going for us is . . . you."

"Me?" Slocum stared at Ned, his confidence waning by the second. "I thought you were going out there, too."

"Oh, I am, but though I know these woods and this here river valley, I don't have a clue as to how to track a man."

"To tell you the truth, Ned, tracking a man in the snow isn't all that difficult." Slocum helped Frenchy stuff the last of the provisions they'd need into the pack basket, then cinched the canvas cover down tight and gave it a few extra knots for safekeeping. It wouldn't do to have their food spill out should he take a tumble on the snowshoes. He'd been on the things a few times in his years roving the West, but never in such terrain, and mixed with a manhunt.

"We'll take the black team downtrail back toward town," said Ned. "That's a good stretch. I'm hoping he'll be somewhere along there, maybe the boys missed him the first time through. But you know what my old father used to say about hope, don't you?"

"I have no idea," said Slocum, "but I'm beginning to see why you and Jigger get along so well."

"Who says we get along? I can't stand the man." Ned laughed. "But then again, he probably can't stand me either. Heh heh."

"So what did your father used to say?"

"Oh, about hope? He'd say, 'Hope in one hand, fill t'other with rocks, and see which fills up faster.'"

"I think I would have liked your father."

"Nah, he was worse than Jigger."

"Oh, I see." Slocum couldn't help smiling. "So are we ready then?"

"Yep, the boys'll have the team watered and fed and rigged. Anson will man the team—that way he can bring them back here if need be. Or on to town, and we can hoof it back."

On their journey down the mountainside, they took the same primary log-driving trail that Slocum had used to get to the Tamarack.

As they slid downtrail, the horses, while not the match of Jigger's Belgians, were powerful pulling beasts, up to the task of hauling loads of logs a whole lot heavier than three men and a bit of gear. The wind came directly at them, funneled through the trough the road had formed in the vale of pines. Slocum felt its cold sting on his cheeks, just above his beard. He kept his mouth clenched tight, but soon he had to rewrap the wool scarf he'd been wearing nearly around the clock, so cold and biting had the temperatures become.

"We're coming close to where the boys say they backtracked and claim they saw sign in the snow as if Jigger had stopped—or someone had stopped the team. I dunno, all we can do is try."

Slocum nodded. "It's as good a place as any to start. We need to get cracking, because nightfall is coming—and sooner in the mountains. And this storm, as you say, is fixing to be a doozy. Once the snow starts for real, following any tracks will be that much more difficult."

But it was still another mile or so until they spotted the "corner boulder," as the men referred to it, because the big gray stone marked a turn in the mountain trail. As Anson slowed the team to a halt before the rock, Slocum hopped down onto the packed road surface. Following each snow, Jigger sent a team of horses and men to drag a snow roller along the surface of the trail to help keep it passable by packing the fresh white stuff atop the old.

It worked pretty well, and the newest skin of snow provided Slocum with a fresh set of confusing tracks. As he bent low to study them, he noted a number of what appeared to be huge wolflike tracks, as well as men's boots and horse prints. Then farther off to the side of the trail, the uphill, mountain valley side, he found snowshoe tracks, made by at least two men, perhaps three—it was difficult to tell, as they were hampered by new falling snow.

"We best get going," said Slocum, pointing into the woods. "Tracks lead that way and there's no time to lose."

Ned nodded and cupped his hands, yelled back to Anson, waiting at the sledge twenty feet away. "Give us ten minutes. If we don't return, you best head back." He turned to Slocum with raised eyebrows, as if to have Slocum verify what he'd just told the young logger with the team.

"That sounds fair," said Slocum, and Ned turned back toward the waiting teamster for confirmation. The man waved back and gave a vigorous nod.

Slocum bent close to Ned's ear and said, "These tracks weren't made by one man. There were at least two, and on snowshoes. I may be wrong, but all sign points to Jigger having been taken."

"Hellfire!" said Ned. "And I bet I know just who's behind it."

"It wouldn't be that Whitaker character, would it?"

"The one and only. I'll fill you in on more about the situation later. I expect you've been kept in the dark long enough."

Slocum wanted to say, "Mighty big of you," but he held his tongue. Maybe they all had good reason for being secretive. Maybe it wasn't anything more than loyalty to Jigger and a respect for keeping the man's affairs private. It didn't really matter to him just now so much as wanting to do all he could to make sure Jigger and his captors, if that was what the situation was, were tracked and found. And fast.

As if to punctuate that thought, a stray, bold gust of icy wind snaked in from the road and buffeted the two men. It pressed their heavy wool mackinaws tight to their backs, made them pull their collars tighter around their faces. Slocum finished strapping on his snowshoes, checked that Ned had done the same, then led the way, bent forward to the task at hand.

Slocum hustled, making as much time as he could following the tracks before he lost light and the tracks to snow. He had no worries about Ned keeping up with him, as the man spent a good deal of time in the contraptions. Slocum was pleased to note that he himself kept upright and didn't falter too much. The trail was easy to follow, but dark was descending.

Soon the hidden land sloped upward and their pace slowed. He gazed farther upslope and saw that their trail cut switchbacks up a steep rise out in the open, some of it uncovered with snow, the white layer having slumped to reveal a talus slope beneath. That gave the pursued away. Slocum had seen such indications plenty of times. Without weight such as from a sheep or a man to undermine the snow, it was unlikely that the layer would have slid of its own accord.

He nodded toward the slope and Ned returned the nod, no doubt seeing the same thing. But then Slocum could see that the trail cut up and over the ridge.

"What's beyond that ridge?"

Ned rubbed a mitten over his beard, softening the ice crystals formed there. "Got a boulder field there, then she picks back on up there where we can't see, with trees and such." He reached for his pipe, but he'd tucked it away in an inner coat pocket when they'd begun their trek. He grinned. "Habit."

Slocum nodded, then having caught his breath, he plunged on ahead. Had to make time before the light dwindled. He wasn't worried about himself and Ned—they had plenty of provisions and Ned was a savvy woodsman—but what happened to Jigger? And why?

They managed to make it to the top of the scree slope, and once they broke out of the tree cover, they gained visibility. The snowshoe tracks, three sets for certain, continued down the other side and on up to the next.

Slocum sped up his pace and just behind him he heard Ned shout, "Easy does it, boy. You snap a leg out here and—"

That was all Slocum heard, for a gunshot ripped the darkening, lead gray sky. It had come so close that Slocum heard the buzz as it sliced the air by his head, felt the very movement of air. Instinct caused him to turn, hunching low, a reflexive move honed from years of trailing and tracking and being trailed and tracked himself. He noted with eyeblink speed that his sleeve now bore a smoking gash. He felt no sting, so he knew it was only his woolen coat that had been grazed.

But not so with Ned. He had stopped speaking so abruptly because he had taken that bullet smack-dab in the middle of his forehead. Slocum had no time to do anything more than drop to his knee, crouching low over the older man, hoping against hope that the shot hadn't been fatal—perhaps he'd been somehow miraculously grazed? But his gut knew better.

He had no time for more such thinking because a second,

then a third shot whipped in low, spanged off jagged rubble around him. He grabbed Ned by the lapels, shouted, "Ned! Come on, man!"

No response, but Slocum hadn't waited for one. He grabbed the front of the man's coat tighter and hurled them both downslope. They tumbled, side over side, Slocum doing his best to hug tight to the man he'd come to regard highly, even in the short time he had known him.

His goal was a large crag of rock twice the height of a man and three times as wide at the base. This, he hoped, if he had judged the direction from which the bullets had come, would provide protection from the shooters, if not protection from the wind. Anything was possible, but that would be too much to hope for.

First, though, they needed to make it down there in one piece. They tumbled like rag-doll men, legs and arms akimbo, slamming into the slope, collecting snow, and jamming into rocks, before finally colliding with the leading edge of the ragged boulder.

Slocum lay still for a moment, his breath coming in short, gagging gouts. If the bullet hadn't killed Ned, then the tumble surely did. It sure as hell hadn't done Slocum any good, of that he was certain. As rough as it had been, as he began to move, he didn't sense any broken bones. He knew he'd be covered in welts and stiff as a board the next day. But it beat being dead.

"Ned?" He held the man's coat by the front once again and, kneeling, raised the man up in front of him. Aside from a fresh cut on the man's cheek, there was no change, and now Slocum could see with certainty that the shot had killed the man instantly, coring right into his forehead as it had. A small blessing, he thought as he lowered Ned to the ground.

Judging by the fact that the shooter hadn't cranked off another round, Slocum guessed they felt they'd accomplished their task and either scared him off their tail or shot them both. Either way, he figured he was in a world of hurt. Whatever had happened to Jigger—and he presumed the scrappy little man was still alive, because of the three sets of snowshoe tracks—he couldn't worry about him now.

He hoped that he was out of the shooter's sight, because with this weather coming in, he had to make a fire, or strap on a pair of angel wings himself. And as cold as his face and hands and feet were, and as chattery as his choppers were, he had no intention of giving in so easily. He'd make a fire close to the rock face, hunker in, and kill anything that came close. But first, he thought, as the mountain night closed quickly, he'd have to figure out how much of their goods from the pack baskets had spilled out onto the snow on the way downslope.

He knew he had lost a snowshoe, and he'd heard a lot of loud clattering—he hoped it hadn't been his rifle snapping in half. But beyond that, he had no idea what sort of shape his gear was in.

17

"Well, if it ain't John Slocum, the dandiest limbin' logger this trapper woman ever has clapped eyes on."

From his dark spot behind his guttering fire, Slocum breathed a low sigh and eased back on the hammer. "Hella. What brings you out on a night like this?"

As he waited for her to approach, he thought, How much do I really know about her anyway? For all he knew, she could be the one who'd made off with Jigger, could be the one who'd drilled Ned and tried to kill him, too.

She must have sensed his hesitation, because in a low, less playful voice, she said, "I saw the men you're tracking. I saw what they did, saw your tumble, too. I'm surprised you're still able to function. I was too far off to be of use. Until now."

"Who says I can function?" he said, not quite ready to reveal all his cards to this stranger—even if she was a handsome one.

"Your friend, Ned, the old logger. They kill him?"

"Yeah. At least he didn't suffer any. It was a quick, clean shot."

"I remember him well. Kind man, from what I could tell." Slocum could hear a tinge of sadness tighten her voice.

"Yeah, nice fella," he said.

"He was McGee's right-hand man, wasn't he?"

"Yep."

"Okay, John Slocum. Just to prove I am what I say, I'm coming in, both hands up, rifle uncocked, gripped high on the barrel where I won't be able to make any fast moves. Got me?"

Slocum thought for a half beat, then said, "No, don't give up your piece—those backshooting bastards might be watching."

He heard her sigh. "John Slocum, as I said, I saw them. And they're long gone. If they were still watching, you wouldn't be listening to me talking right now because I wouldn't be talking right now. At least not to you. I'm not dumb enough to walk into a firefight uninvited."

Slocum smirked—she had a point. "Who would you be talking with, then?"

"Oh, I expect I'd be sitting alone in my cabin, thinking up some way to amuse myself."

"Must get lonely," he said as she came up to the fire and knelt on the other side, her hands extended out over the flames.

"Yep," she said.

In the low, flickering light, she looked even prettier than he remembered. Either that or the weather was already playing tricks on him. He leaned forward. "You said you saw the men I'm tracking. How many were there?"

"I expect you know the answer to that, but I'll indulge you. There were three. Two goons who work for Whitaker, near as I can figure, and they had Jigger between them. From a distance it looked as if he took a nasty knock to the bean, which would explain why he was so quiet. From what I know about Jigger, if he was being hoo-raahed or corralled by anyone, he'd be livelier than a scalded cat and twice as loud."

Slocum nodded, appreciating the information, but wanting more. "You know which direction they headed, so point it out to me. I might be able to gain on them tonight before the snow piles up much more."

She snorted. "You have to be kidding, Mr. John Slocum. This storm? You'd be lucky to make it over that next rise without dying of frostbite. Or getting addled and turned around five times."

"I have to do something. They killed Ned, they have Jigger, for what reason I'm still unsure of, and they tried to kill me."

"I know all that. But take it easy. I happen to know where they're going. I also happen to know that once they get there, they won't be going anywhere for a couple of days."

"How do you know all this?"

"Because they're headed to a line shack trappers use—sometimes I use it when I'm feeling too lazy to head back to my place."

"How do you know they're going there?"

"Because I was there a couple of days ago, checking on things. I knew a storm was coming in soon and I always make a point of checking on it before the big snows barrel in. I noticed it had been stocked up with all sorts of things I wouldn't have put there, and I'm pretty much the only trapper left up here nowadays anyway. So when I saw those men with Jigger today making a beeline in that direction, I figured I knew where they'd end up. I never expected to see them, let alone to see them shooting at someone fogging their backtrail. And that turned out to be you and poor Ned."

Slocum was about to respond when she spoke again. "I was too far away to help. Or I would have, I hope you know." She looked up at him, her eyes shining with tears that he was sure she wouldn't let flow. "I would have dropped them in their tracks."

"I know it, Hella. And thanks."

She straightened. "Now that you know it would be a fool's errand to head out after them in this storm, and in the dark, let's get out of here."

Despite the situation, Slocum laughed and stood, wincing as he felt the first pull of what he knew would be many knots and aches. "Just where do you propose we 'get' to?"

"My cabin. It's a whole lot closer than the one they're headed for, and a whole lot warmer than this damn rock you're huddled under."

"I'll need to bring Ned."

"We certainly can," she said. "But we'd only have to bring him back this way once the storm passes, which might be tomorrow, might be in two days."

"I don't want any critters after him."

"Not much worry of that. Only critters foolish enough to be out here in this storm are humans. We'll bundle him up, leave him laid out here in the lee of this rock. I'd only have to do the same at my place."

"Fair enough," said Slocum, not having to think too much about it. They readied Ned's body, knowing that when they returned to bring him to town, he'd be stiff as a log himself. Then Slocum made one good pair of snowshoes out of the three shoes left, shrugged into his pack basket, hefted the other, and they headed out. Hella led the way, a rope tied to her waist trailing back a few yards to Slocum's belt, where he'd tied his end.

"I know the way in the dark," she shouted into his ear.

"Good thing!" he replied.

Once they stepped away from the boulder, the storm drove at them like a fist, blinding and incessant in its attack.

18

True to her word, within an hour's hard march, Hella led them straight to her cabin. Slocum had kept up with her, and the trek felt good, kept his already sore limbs from seizing up, as they surely would have in the cold by that boulder. He thought of Ned, a good man laid low for what reason, Slocum had little idea. It involved some fool named Whitaker, of that much he was certain, and Jigger was the target of sorts.

Short of a justified revenge killing, Slocum could see little reason for those men shooting Ned in the head and trying to kill Slocum, as well. He'd find them tomorrow, and force the explanation out of them, one snapping bone at a time, if he had to. It hadn't been his fight, but now that they had shot a friend and tried to do the same to him, by God, they'd made it his fight. And John Slocum wouldn't take that from anyone.

A high-pitched growling scream rose from the darkness off to their immediate right. And close, too damn close. Slocum's neck hairs shot straight out like quills. He knew exactly what it was—the skoocoom—and he hated it, mostly because here he was, a grown man, and it had become all too real, too close, and too personal for him not to believe in.

It was something, after all. Something in the dark made those noises and owned those damnable glowing eyes and left those mammoth footprints and tore the piss out of that storage shed. Something, and it might as well have the name of skoocoom.

"Is that what I think it is?" he said, leaning close to her.

"Skoocoom, yep," she said, not even breaking stride. "Leave 'em be and they'll leave us be."

Another, deeper growl, sudden in its attack and snapping intensity, burst from the dark just to the other side of the trail. Slocum could swear it was close enough for him to touch. And that meant the thing was close enough to touch him. But from what he'd seen, these brutes wouldn't just touch something. Their idea of touching meant tearing it apart. He had no doubts it could rip the limbs from his body, kick him, and stomp him to death. Hell, maybe even try to eat him.

He cranked the hammer back on his Colt. The sound brought Hella to a sudden stop. She wheeled around, so close he felt her breath on his face.

"What are you doing?" she hissed.

"They start something, I intend to finish it. Or die trying."

"They're not going to do anything. As long as you're with me anyway."

"How does that work? You friendly with them?"

She turned around, began marching again. Off to either side of them, Slocum heard heavy breaths, thought he could detect swinging movements in the dark, heard random grunts and the snapping of branches.

"In a manner of speaking, I guess we're on friendly terms, yeah. Just calm down about it and it'll all be fine.

Okay? Otherwise, we die here and now and never get the chance to save Jigger."

Slocum sighed, kept on walking. "Okay, okay," he said, but didn't ease off the hammer on the Colt. He kept the revolver in his hand, and nothing would convince him to holster it.

"John Slocum!"

The voice came from ahead and he realized she had stopped. How much time had passed? He knew the skoocoom sounds had stopped sometime back, as if the things had become bored with them. He almost bumped into her. He straddled the backs of her snowshoes with his and stepped in close behind her. "Are we at your place?"

He could barely see a yard in front of them, so thickly was the snow now falling.

"Yep. Home sweet home," she said, bending down before him and unstrapping her snowshoes.

He backed up and did the same. The only way he could tell where the cabin sat was by the sound of her snowshoes clunking against the logs.

"Up here," she said. "Hang them on the hooks so they don't get buried under a drift."

He felt his way along the wall, felt her snowshoes hanging, then a free hook—a length of branch forming a holder protruding from a log. He groped along the wall and found she was waiting for him a couple of feet away. "Come on in," she said in a shout.

As soon as she opened the door, Slocum felt immediate relief. Where moments before there had been pitch blackness stitched with the pelting whiteness of snow, now there was the low glow of a warming fire cradled in a beautifully built stone hearth. The tang of wood smoke was dappled with something at once comforting and calming—cinnamon and clove perhaps? It reminded him of long-ago winter evenings at the family hearth, good winter nights when even in the South, where he was raised, the temperatures would dip down and they would all crowd close, talking of the day's work, thankful to be close and warm on frigid dark nights.

"Make yourself at home, Mr. John Slocum."

"You don't have to call me that, you know."

"Isn't that your name?" she said, smiling and shrugging out of her coat.

"Yeah," he said, sinking down to his knees before the fire and prodding it back into life with an old wooden cane, the curved handle worn smooth as a ram's horn, the end a charred nub from fire poking. He laid a length of wood on and blew on the coals. It crackled and he turned to see Hella approaching with a Dutch oven. She set it on an iron arm that swung out over the flames.

"That should help take the edge off the cold. It'll take a while to warm up, I'm afraid. Same with the coffee."

"That's fine. I appreciate your hospitality. I have nowhere else to go. Not until tomorrow anyway."

"Or until the storm lets up."

"Yep," he said, standing and wincing from the thrashing he'd taken in the long downslope tumble. "As long as it lets up tomorrow."

"You are a stubborn one, aren't you? Threatening nature to bend to your will. That's mighty bold, Mr. Slocum."

"Call me John. And yes, I'm bold. But only when it comes to tracking down mankillers and kidnappers."

"Well, we're well situated to head on out after them. That line cabin they're holed up in is to the east by two ravines. But if you're going to be of any use in a fight, you had better shuck out of those sodden clothes and dry them by the fire. You have any dry clothes in that pack basket?"

"Nah, my longhandles will be dry, I expect."

"Fine, hand me those wet things, I'll get them drying."

Slocum looked around for a place to perch so he could

tug off his boots, but there was only one chair, and it was already stacked with other gear.

"Sit on the bed there and I'll help you with your boots."

"Oh, no need for that, Hella. I can . . ." But as he bent to pull off the boots, he felt as if he were a century old, and stiff as a stick.

She leaned over him, pushing him back to a sitting position, and that was when he noticed that she'd pared down her own clothing to baggy wool trousers and a button-down wool shirt, green-and-black-checked, which was unbuttoned low enough that the V of the shirt parted to reveal the soft, smooth curves of what looked to Slocum to be perfect breasts. He let his weary eyes linger there, taking in the pretty sight just a smidge too long. He cut his gaze up to hers, and she smiled down at him, shaking her head as if she'd just caught him sneaking pennies from a church basket.

She backed away as he sank to his elbows, still watching her. She turned around, straddled his right leg, her backside facing him. Grasping his boot, she tugged and tugged and finally it came sliding off. Without looking at him, she did the same with the left. Then tugged the bottoms of his pant legs. This was his cue to unbuckle his belt and unbutton his denims, which he did. She tugged and slid them off, one leg at a time, did the same with his socks, then carried all his gear to the fire. He peeled off his own shirt and lay back on his elbows on the bed, sleepily watching her arrange his clothes before the fire.

When she came back, she once again turned her back to him, straddled both his legs this time, and began slowly, gently, but with a firmness that only comes from strong hands, massaging his tired legs. She worked her way up his legs, backward, from his calves to his knees, then thighs, still with her backside facing him.

It was only then that he noticed that somewhere she'd lost the shapeless wool trousers. As she bent to her task of massaging his legs, her wool shirt rode up enough to reveal her bare backside, smooth cheeks with a touch of red from the cold. He longed to reach out and touch her there.

She worked his legs, fervently and with a whole-body effort, inching ever closer to his waist. As she dipped down again, leaning low, he was treated to a clear view from between her rosy cheeks straight through a lovely thatch of golden hair, and to her jostling breasts hanging and swinging with each renewed effort of massage she gave him.

By this time, his longhandles, a faded pink instead of the bright red as when new, had begun to rise in the middle, pushing the fabric upward. The only thing he knew to do was unbutton them from the top down to where the buttons ended, just before her still-bobbing backside. Once freed, his member sprang upright, unencumbered.

Hella must have sensed this because she began to back ever higher up his legs. Soon he was bumped tight to her back. She lifted the shirt, which had somehow become unbuttoned in the process, and let it slide down her shoulders, and halfway down her back. Then she rose up and in one smooth movement lowered herself onto him, plunging herself downward slowly, a long breath, like quiet steam, escaping through her mouth.

The shirt slid down farther and she slipped one arm out, then the other, and tossed the shirt aside. Still straddling him, but on her knees on the bed, and facing the room and the fireplace at the far end, she rose up and down with slow, sure ease. They both shuddered at the full and immense pleasure this simple act offered.

She leaned back slightly and Slocum reached around under her arms and covered her breasts with his hands, gently massaging them with his callused palms. She groaned and reached down, playing with him at the same time. Their momentum increased with their increasing warmth, and though she was still facing away from him, she bucked and rode him as though he were trying to throw her. Soon her back arched and tensed, the skin glowing with a thin sheen of sweat.

Slocum saw the defined hard muscles of her back, her shoulders, her arms and neck, whenever her long gold hair swayed side to side. Finally she stopped altogether, every one of those muscles tight with anticipation of the hot relief that was due to them any second.

And they didn't have long to wait. The feisty trapper's back worked up and down, side to side, making it a lovely thing to watch, nearly as nice as the vigor with which she grasped him without touching him with her hands. It seemed to him that she wasn't done, and sure enough, she began riding him again. But first, she raised a leg and spun clear around on him, so that she faced him.

She bent low and ran her hands all over his hairy chest, gently massaging him, just as he did to her backside. And they rode on like that for quite a while.

Just at the point when they were both breathing hard and ready for a break, she raised her face up off his chest and said, "Stew's ready." She slid off him slowly, as if hating to do so, slipped on the wool shirt, still unbuttoned, and padded over to the fireplace.

Slocum lay there for a few moments more, then she said, "You better get up, because while I will do a whole lot of things in life, one of them ain't serving a man food in bed."

She winked and he smiled and he buttoned up his longhandles and made his way to the fireplace, where they had hot stew, and hotter coffee. Then when they'd finished there, they crawled back into bed, this time under the covers, and rode like hell for a good while longer.

19

Morning came for Slocum far earlier than daylight. He heard only a slight wind, low but insistent, but not the persistent pelting of snow. As if reading his mind, Hella spoke in the dark beside him. "Sounds like the snow stopped, but the wind didn't."

"Still," said Slocum, "it's a lot quieter sounding than last night."

He wanted to be up and ready, and out tracking the culprits of all this misery, as early as possible. To his relief, Hella roused him through quick, deft ministrations with her warm, strong hands, convincing him without words that they had plenty of time before they had to depart.

Later, satisfied that they each had performed a fair amount of pre-rising activity, they greeted the chill morning air with hurried steps to the fireplace, used the thunderpot, and tugged on their day's clothes in a hurry, lest they somehow lose the heat they had worked up within their bodies.

And thus, in short order, Slocum and Hella found themselves on the trail, or what she told him was the trail. It proved to be nothing more than a line that wound its way through the trees much like any other potential course that Slocum could pick out. But he trusted she knew where to go. She had practically been born in these mountains, after all.

They didn't talk much on the way upward, deeper, and at times higher. Sometimes they angled downward, though always heading in a switchback fashion higher into the hills. And as they trekked, the wind increased. Into their second hour, a dark, cloudy mass became visible. As it rolled over the top of the ridge far above them, Hella held up her rifle in a doeskin-mittened hand, then half turned to Slocum, who was right on her tail.

"That"—she jerked her head toward the looming dark mass—"doesn't look good. It looks to be carrying with it a whole new batch of snow. We don't have much further to go to get to the cabin, but it's going to be tricky getting back out of there."

Slocum squinted up at it. "How much further?"

"See that fold there?"

He nodded.

"Just the other side of it sits the cabin. Tucked in just above a wash, backed by pines and protected by boulders. It's a good halfway point to decent hunting and trapping grounds."

Slocum nodded again. "I have an idea."

"Uh-oh," she said. "When a man says that, someone somewhere—usually a woman—gets the short end of the stick."

He grinned. "Nothing like that. But I do think you should let me go on alone." He held up a quieting hand when she began to protest. "Hear me out now. I need you to go back to the Tamarack. I expect you can cut across country faster than me. I'm going to need help hauling those two on out of there, plus we don't know what sort of shape Jigger's going to be in. Not to mention we'll have to haul Ned's body on out of the hills, too."

She stared hard at him. Finally she said, "I understand what you're saying, Slocum. But it's bull and you know it. You're like all the other men who think they're doing a girl a favor by protecting her from trouble. Well, I'm not like any of those other girls, you understand me?"

"I know you're not. And you're probably right. I guess there was some part of me that wanted to keep you from getting shot at. But only because I've spent the better part of my life tracking lowdown dogs like these men, and I know that when they're cornered, they're as likely to shoot as a snake is to strike."

"I hear that. Don't forget I earn my keep, such as it is, by trapping critters and making meat of others. Only taking what I need, mind you."

"Outlaws are a whole lot different than trapped beavers, though." Slocum was getting the sense that all his arguing wasn't about to change her mind. She stared at him and he felt his resolve peter out. She was probably handy with that rifle anyway. He just hoped she stayed well hidden and was savvy enough not to try anything stupid. Unlike what he knew he would have to do . . .

As if to say, "Then it's settled," she plunged on ahead. "We need to get there before that snow cloud dumps down."

It didn't take too long before Slocum found himself once again bumping into her, but this time she held her other mitten to her muffled face and in a low voice said, "There she is."

Slocum followed her gaze and had to squint at the jumble of snow-covered boulders and the tapering mass of spiking trees for a few moments before he made out the snake of sooty smoke threading up from behind a nearby rise before whipping away once the breeze reached it.

"I see it now," he said. "Where's the door?"

"The west side. It's a half soddy, sort of built into the hillside."

Slocum looked at her, then at the house, then back at her.

"You thinking what I'm thinking?" she said with a wink.

"If you're thinking that we might be able to block the chimney, smoke them out, then yep, we're thinking the same thing."

"I weigh less, might not be noticed," she said.

Slocum wasn't sure how he felt about sending her up there, but time was running short and he had no alternatives. And then a creaking sounded, followed by a loud clunking noise. The cabin door had slammed open. Then a gunshot echoed down the valley and that made the decision for him. They both dropped to the snow, rifles held poised before them. Presently they heard shouts, one voice rising above the other.

"You sumbitch! I ain't never cheated in all my days and you claiming I done that? No sir! No sir, I say!" The voice rose to a reedy pitch and sounded familiar to Slocum. He poked his head up out of the snow and saw a tall, thin man waving a revolver.

The man was clad only in longhandles, flopping untied boots, and a stocking cap perched at a lopsided angle on his head. Behind the man, the cabin door lolled open, hanging sideways like a crooked tooth in the smile that was the cabin front. The tall man weaved on his feet, his head looking as if it were held up by a tugged string.

From the dim interior of the cabin, a deeper bellow of a voice shouted, "Shut that damn door or you'll have a whole lot more to worry about than me calling you a cheat!"

The thin man weaved in a circle, his revolver seeming to weigh his arm down, before bouncing back up again. He cranked back on the hammer and fired a second shot, this time back at the cabin front. "You shut your mouth! You called me a cheat, but you got no right! No right!"

Slocum dropped back down and in a low voice said, "At least we know for certain they're here."

"Hard to miss," she said. "Now if we only knew about Jigger."

"One way to find out." Slocum rose up on his knees, scouting like a prairie dog. He noted that the man inside didn't appear inclined to get up to retrieve his friend, let alone shut the door, so he was either lazy or preoccupied or drunk. No matter, the thin one—Slocum was sure he was the same thin, whining man who'd helped attack him back on his first day at the Tamarack Camp—was also not showing any sign of heading back inside. He guessed the gargle he'd had, and from the looks of him he'd had quite a few shares, made him somewhat impervious to the cold.

Slocum knelt back down with his face close to Hella's. "If I can get him out of the line of vision of that open door, but without him yelping to give us away, might be we can take him hostage."

"Leave it to me—but you hide right there. He'll come over here, and when he does, you nab him."

"How are you—" But he didn't have to guess for much longer, for she had whipped open her coat, lifted the bulky sweater beneath, unbuttoned layers of shirts, and finally parted her longhandle top to reveal her beautiful breasts. She stood there in the breeze, the cold making her fingertip-size nipples stand erect as frozen raspberries. She winked down at Slocum, who'd backed away just out of sight behind the sculpted drift to her right.

Then she made a sexy clicking noise with her mouth, as if urging a horse to do her bidding. The skinny drunk's head spun as if on a pulley, finally settled on what Slocum guessed the man must have thought was a stunning dream.

When she was sure he had seen all she appeared to be promising, Hella hooked a beckoning finger at him. The man turned once back to the doorway of the cabin, then looked back at her. She shook her head no, and the intention was obvious—just him, not anyone else. The drunken man staggered forward, as if he were a parched desert traveler and she were a tall glass of cool beer, her glassy sides beading with tempting promise.

A smile cracked his face and he yelped, "Yee-haaa!" and lurched toward her, staggering through the wind-stiffened snow.

His shout made Slocum wince inside. If the man in the cabin chose to get up, he'd see her, and might not take as kindly to the unexpected visitor, no matter how pleasant or tempting her offerings might be. Luckily the man inside still didn't budge, and the thin man held his peace, having realized there was the pesky problem of snow between him and the breasty dream. He staggered forward.

Hella kept her wide smile pasted on, her eyes fixed on him, but out of the corner of her mouth she spoke low, so Slocum could hear, "Hurry up, asshole . . . my girls are about frosted over!"

It was all Slocum could do to keep from barking out a laugh. Just a few more steps and the man would be well enough away from the sight line of the cabin door, then Slocum could nab him. A few more . . .

When he was still a good man-length from her, the thin drunk dove forward, his cold-reddened hands curving into claws before him, one still gripping the revolver. His boot toes caught in the snow and he pitched forward. Slocum drove down on top of him, grabbing for the man's throat with one hand and with the other scrabbling in the snow to snatch up the revolver.

He managed to do both while Hella dropped down and drove a knee into the drunk's face. His cries of pain and surprise mingled but were choked off by both Slocum's deadly grip and Hella's forceful knee. She buttoned her layers of shirts, pulled down the sweater, and with a sigh and a shudder, refastened the buttons on the coat.

In the meantime, Slocum managed to deliver three quick, sharp jabs to the man's temple, jaw, and nose, rendering the thin drunk unconscious. He dragged him down behind the drift, trussed him like a turkey dressed for the oven, and wrapped a kerchief gag tight around his mouth and cheeks. The man might well be heard above the building of the wind and snowstorm, but probably not until they had gained entrance to the cabin . . . somehow.

20

"That should keep him quiet." Slocum rose from his knees, peering toward the cabin door. It was doubtful that anyone inside could see anywhere in his direction. Now all they had to do was wait for the man inside the cabin to come on out, wondering where in the hell his friend had gotten to. Slocum was sure it was the same one whose nose he'd rearranged.

Hella sidestepped over closer to Slocum as he dragged the unconscious drunk farther behind the drift.

"You think he'll come out?" she said.

"I hope so. I'd love a clear shot at him."

"Exactly what I'd do—kill him first, ask questions later."

"Not quite what I had in mind. I figured I'd wing him enough to get him to drop his weapon, then rush him. Well, rush him as much as this snow will allow. Of course"—he smiled and continued whispering—"we could always show him your—"

"Watch your language, Mr. Slocum." She winked as she said it.

He nodded, indicating past her toward the cabin, from which they heard a shout.

"Where in the hell did you get to? You said you was going to go write your name in the snow. Hell, the letter X ain't that long! Course, I know you can't write worth a bean." He laughed long and loud, guffawing as if he'd told a real knee-slapper. "You don't get in here quick and shut that damn door, I'm going to come out there and shoot you in the head, leave you for dead. I'll get all the money and you won't get nothing but that lead pill to suckle on for eternity."

"He's a windy bastard," Hella said.

Slocum nodded, said nothing. He suspected the man would come out any second. Or at least make it to the door.

"Should we just hurry up his game and smoke him out?"

"Not yet. Be better if we wait him out. Any second now." Slocum raised his rifle to his shoulder. They both tensed. Between them on the ground, the stricken, bound man twitched slightly but didn't yet revive.

"Oh, for Pete's sake," she said. Before Slocum could grab her, Hella had kicked through the snow on her snowshoes upslope, then onto the undisturbed roof of the cabin protruding from the hillside. She stepped onto it, gingerly setting her weight down ahead of her, one step at a time, while Slocum swiveled his gaze from the cabin's still-open front door to the roof, where she was slowly advancing to the stone chimney that jutted from the western edge, partially against the back wall.

He wanted to shout at her, wanted to throttle her for being so hasty. He felt sure the man was about to wander out in a drunken stupor, then Slocum would have him, and the whole game would be done as far as he knew—unless they met a friend up here, someone else in on the kidnapping. That was a possibility.

He was also bothered by the fact that he'd not heard a peep from Jigger. Could be they'd tied him up, kept him trussed so tight he wasn't able to speak. Could also be that he was dead, though that seemed less likely, other than due to an accident, since they'd gone to all this trouble to kidnap the man. And then haul him all the way up here? For what, though? Ransom?

None of that mattered just now. Slocum had to make sure that Hella didn't get shot through the roof. It seemed, from what little he could see of the edge, that it was a stout structure with pole rafters and mosses and branches laid over that. But that didn't mean there weren't spots where the layers had thinned, making it all too easy to let the snow drift on down. A skittish outlaw would surely crank off a round or two straight up into the ceiling, just in case.

"Hey!" he heard the man inside shout. "What you doing up on the roof?"

Slocum tensed. He cut his eyes to Hella. She had paused, just a couple feet shy of the smoking chimney. Luckily the wind had dwindled a bit, but the new snow had begun to fall faster and thicker, clinging to Slocum's hat brim, the side of his face, his shoulders, his rifle.

Then the thing Slocum had just feared might happen did happen—he heard two rapid shots from inside, saw white powder blaze upward from the roof, one plume blossoming two feet behind Hella, the other closer in. He didn't think it got her, because she jackrabbited as soon as the second shot sounded, and launched herself at the chimney. She hugged it with one arm, ripping at her coat with the other arm and managing to shrug out of it. Then she lay the heavy garment over the chimney before tucking into a roll and launching herself off the far side of the roof.

She disappeared from Slocum's sight, but he was already on the move, hustling toward the cabin front and praying there wasn't a side door that opened out toward where she'd no doubt landed, hopefully unhurt and already clawing her own side arm out of its holster.

"I get you, asshole?" the man inside cackled. "I sure hope so. Been thinkin' about it and I like the idea of having all the money for my own self. You can go to hell on a fast horse."

"Some friend you are!" Slocum shouted from just outside the door, hoping the man inside bought Slocum's effort at making his voice sound like that of the unconscious thin drunk.

"That you?"

He sounded genuinely worried and not a little disappointed.

Slocum decided to push his luck. He had to get to Hella, after all, and there was no way he could stand there yammering with this fool. All he really wanted to do was rush in there and shoot the jackass in the head, but that wouldn't solve a thing except put himself, and maybe even Jigger, in dire danger.

"You gonna have to come on in here if'n you want me, stranger!" The man fairly roared the proclamation and Slocum knew he'd been discovered. He pulled back for a moment, considered what his next move should be—he hoped Hella was okay over there on the other side of the cabin. He trusted she was, and hoped the snow was thick enough where she'd dropped that there was nothing there to injure her. But that would have to be a secondary concern. Right now he had bigger fish to fry. "You might as well know we have you surrounded, mister!"

A long pause, then the man said, "I'm not so sure I believe you. What of my friend?"

"He's been taken prisoner and is right now singing like a bird about your plans."

"Again, I'm not so sure of anything you say. Might be I'll just go ahead and shoot this old man right now."

"What old man would that be?" said Slocum, hurriedly unstrapping his snowshoes, hoping to buy more time until he could figure out how to get in there without getting himself killed.

A shotgun blast from inside booming outward toward the door decided for him. The frame pulsed and jagged strips of wood flew outward. "Take that, asshole!" Again, the man roared with laughter. Though not quite as loud as his shotgun, his voice nevertheless was loud enough for every creature anywhere near the valley to hear.

Slocum figured that if he ducked low, aimed high, and fired a few rounds, he might be able to get inside. The woman would just have to wait—or fend for herself. She was quite capable of doing that, as she'd already proven.

He thumbed back the hammer on the Colt Navy, did the same with his rifle, and dropping down to one knee, fired as he'd intended—from low to high, up toward the dark space over whoever had his head upright in there.

The smoke from the shotgun blast still rolled outward, and his own blasts really made a thick, smoky soup of things. It also gave Slocum cover enough to scramble inside. There was space to the left of the door, just inside. If it wasn't filled with gear or a bunk, he might be able to roll into the corner and regain a few precious seconds to let his eyes adjust. He was up against a drunk killer, after all, a man who was perfectly willing to kill his own friend and partner in this crazy escapade. He was someone who'd no doubt rather kill than be taken alive or wounded.

"What in the hell is going on?" The man screamed the question from somewhere in the back of the small cabin, off to Slocum's right. It wasn't as dark in there as Slocum had expected, and he could detect the lingering smell of lamp oil, as though someone had just doused the flame. Slocum held his position, waiting for his eyes to adjust and for the smoke to part.

At least enough to let him deliver one true shot. This vermin demanded to be put down. If he didn't kill him, he might be able to learn from him just what in the hell was going on. But if he killed him, Slocum figured he could live with that. He was sore, tired, cranky, and had had enough of these mountains and all the crazy loggers, one Crazy Trapper Lady who didn't listen, and crazy animal men that might or might not exist.

Just as he was set to make a move around the far left wall, sensing as much as seeing a large wide cupboard of some sort there in the dark before him, he heard a voice from the doorway. "John? John Slocum? You okay?"

It was the girl. And dammit, he wasn't the only one who'd heard her.

Slocum hissed, "Get back!" but his words were blown apart with the roar of a second blast from the shotgun. The doorway took the brunt of it again. Smoke and snow and wood and sod erupted in a bigger cloud this time. Had she been hit? No time to find out. But Slocum took the opportunity to cut to the chase.

He drove forward, straight across the cabin, from the front left corner to the back right, from where the blast had come. He didn't dare shoot directly at the blast, because the man might be hiding behind a trussed-up Jigger, but he might have enough time to barrel straight into him.

The smoke clogged Slocum's throat, burned his nostrils, and set his ears to ringing as if his head were filled with pealing church bells. But such situations were not foreign to Slocum. He knew that he would drive forward, unrelenting, pummeling his way in. And that was just what he did.

It took him less than the time it takes to draw a breath to cross the room before the smoke cleared. He plowed into someone, and within a second he knew it was his target and not Jigger, because the someone he plowed into struck back at him, lashing outward with a hard thrashing jab, ramming the butt of a gun just under Slocum's jaw.

Slocum shifted when he felt it and managed to reduce a potentially painful welt into a grazing. It stung, but he had a whole lot more to worry about at the moment than that.

"Gaah!" shouted the shotgun-wielding brute. "You son of a—"

But he didn't get to finish the sentiment because Slocum drove the butt of his Colt Navy straight into the spot where the words were coming from—and struck gold. Slocum felt the fool's teeth snapping, the man's head whipped backward, and as he continued pushing forward, the back of Slocum's gloved hand smeared the man's nose. It gave way in a soft, pulpy spray—it had to be the same man whose nose he'd broken days before—that reminded Slocum of punching a clot of hard-boiled eggs. That was all it took, for the man folded like a deck of cards, fell away from Slocum into the darkness of the corner.

Where the hell was Jigger McGee? Slocum had to find him, but first he had to make damn sure this bastard was disarmed before the brute touched off another blast from his shotgun.

"Slocum? John?"

It was Hella, and he didn't have much more to offer her than "I'm here!" before a coughing fit rattled his lean frame as he dove into the dark corner, fists and guns forward. He still didn't dare deliver a shot, afraid he'd hit Jigger, though that fear was diminishing with each second that passed.

Something hooked him behind an ankle and Slocum felt himself slipping backward. But at the same instant, the smoke parted enough that he saw the object of his attack— the dim outline of a man, crabbing away on his back, clad in longhandles, braces flopping, and wool trousers tangling about his ankles. Slocum guessed while all this hubbub was going on, the man had been trying to don his trousers, but didn't get far enough before Slocum barged in. The men must have been liquoring it up and playing cards when Hella and Slocum arrived.

"You son of a—"

"You said that before!" Slocum shouted, driving his rifle

butt downward. *Slam!* "Now I'm going to have to ask you to stop"—*slam!*—"insulting my dear, departed mother like that!" *Slam!*

Still, the man took the pain, no doubt his liquored-up body absorbing each pummeling blow. Slocum held the rifle aside and backed up a step, drawing his Colt. He was about to tell the man to raise his hands and stand up when from behind his back the bloodied brute produced a skinning knife, drew back with it.

Slocum had just enough time to duck to one side and squeeze the trigger. He sent the first shot into the man's throat. The next followed on its heels, a little higher, boring a smoking trail right through the man's chin. It traveled on up through the center of his head before bursting outward in a flower of blood, bone, and gray ooze, painting the dim log shack's wall with the last of the man's memories. The skinning knife dropped to his lap, his bloodied hand atop it.

Slocum stayed low and to one side, heard an urgent bark from the doorway. Hella again. He coughed and tried to speak, but his throat felt stuffed with sawdust and wool rags. He swallowed, tried again. "I'm okay! Chimney—take the coat off!"

He heard footsteps retreat, and he headed for the doorway himself. No way could he stay in that smoky hellhole. He'd have to wait for it to clear out before he reentered and tried to find Jigger. If he was even in there.

Slocum staggered out the blasted-to-bits doorway, leaning there for a moment before stepping farther out into the bluster of the building storm. The snow felt good on his face, and he tried to lick flakes off his mustache, but it didn't amount to much. He gobbled down a few hand scoops of snow and sighed as the cool stuff melted down into his throat, an elixir better than any he'd ever tasted.

"Where's Jigger?" the woman yelled from the roof.

Slocum was greedily gulping down a mouthful of snow,

so he jerked a thumb over his shoulder, toward the lightly smoking, blasted-out doorway. In truth, he didn't know if the old man was in there or not. He'd not heard a peep from Jigger, but it worked in getting Hella down off the roof and scrambling around the side of the building to help.

"He might be in there—it was too dark and smoky to see."

She nodded as he headed back in, coughing almost as soon as he set foot in the doorway.

She followed him, also offered up a cough. "Jigger! Jigger McGee, you old no-count chicken-legged man, where you at?"

Slocum smiled, despite the situation.

They searched every corner of the cabin while Slocum grabbed the dead man under the arms and dragged him outside. By the time he got him over to the drift where his unconscious partner resided, Slocum had a surprise waiting for him.

"Well, I'll be damned," he said, staring at the snowy trough where the first kidnapper had been laid, trussed up and out cold. The man was not there. The rawhide wraps were there, but that was all. A meandering trail led away and downcountry through the snow. He'd have to wait. Jigger had to be found. Maybe they'd killed him along the way and left him to be covered over in the snow . . .

As he made his way back to the cabin, something told Slocum that wasn't the case. The old man had seemed too important to the two killers. He found Hella standing hipshot, her hands on her waist, looking steamed, hurling a look of annoyance at every corner of the room.

"He has to be here someplace . . . " Then her eyes fixed on the back wall, on which were smeared the remains of the man's head. She smiled. "That's the spot."

"Yeah," said Slocum. "Nothing to be proud of, though. I killed a man."

"No, I mean I bet that's where he's at—I completely forgot there's a root cellar back there behind a small door in the wall. It's dug right into the hillside."

Slocum thumbed a match and coaxed a flame alive in the oil lamp on the plank table. He snatched up the lamp's bail and joined Hella at the bloody back wall.

"There," she said, biting off the end of her chopper mitten, then scrabbling for a fingerhold along the narrow gap. "Used to be a handle, but it looks like someone broke it off."

"We know who." Slocum unsheathed his hip knife and managed to pry open the short door.

Hella held the lamp inside the small opening. "Jigger?" She crawled in on her knees. "Jigger! Slocum, he's here. He doesn't look so good, though. Here, take this." She thrust the lamp at him, then slowly backed out.

Slocum heard a sliding sound and out emerged Hella's backside. She was slowly dragging something backward out of the hole. Out came Jigger, stretched on his back, still wearing his bulky clothes thankfully, but bound at the wrists and ankles with strong, tight rope. His face was unbound, but under his beard the old man's cheeks were sunken and gray and bore purple welts. Trails of dried blood braided his forehead.

"Is he breathing?"

She knelt close, bent her ear to Jigger's upturned mouth. Finally she nodded. "Barely. He's probably half-frozen."

Slocum took that as a cue to coax a renewed fire out of the box stove. In seconds new flames had jumped to life.

"I don't think we can move him out of here, not with that storm coming."

"Let's worry about that once we get him warmed up and we can see what we're dealing with," said Slocum.

As if someone had just nudged him awake, the old man moaned and made a few quiet snorting noises, began to rock his head from side to side.

"John, he's coming around." Hella cradled the old man's head in her lap. "He was always sweet on me, I think. But he's almost my father's age. They were good friends. I think Jigger always envied my father."

"Why's that?" said Slocum, feeding the fire.

"Because Papa never had money problems, at least not the size of the ones Jigger's always battled. But that's only because Pap never cared to own much. Whatever he had, he passed on to me when he died—and that's not saying much. It amounted to traps, the cabin, a deed that might or might not tell what land he owned, and the usual things—pots and pans and such. Jigger's life had become complicated with the logging and having employees and lots more."

"You . . ." The sound came from the old man. Although the word was soft and poorly formed, he was trying hard to speak.

They both took that as a promising sign, and within minutes Slocum had a fine blaze of heat worked up. The cabin's door was beyond easy repair, so staying put had become less of an option.

"As soon as he's up for it, we need to get back to the safety of your cabin. It's a whole lot closer to where we need to be than here. And then I can get out on the trail and find that other fella."

"What? You don't mean the one we tied up?"

"Yep, he escaped." Slocum held up a hand. "Don't ask me how, but he did. He won't get far, though. I expect I'll find him dead. I'll try to find him before that happens, though. Then he can give us some answers."

Jigger sputtered again, then in a low, raspy whisper, finally said, "Good Lordy, will you both quit talking about me as if I ain't here? If we're gonna git going out of this hole in the snow, we'd better get at it while we can."

Hella and Slocum looked at each other, smiling. Not only

was it a relief that Jigger was alive, but it was a double relief because he appeared to be back to his own normal self.

"Besides," said Jigger, "I got to get back to town. Bad things are brewing and I don't want the Tamarack Camp, nor any of my people, to suffer because of it. If Whitaker wants a fight with me, then so be it. But me and me alone. Now let's get going."

Before Hella and Slocum could stop him, Jigger tried to scramble to his feet. He made it halfway upright, but slumped back against the wall, holding his head. "Ahh, spinnin' . . . "

"They hit him a good one," said Hella. "John, let's hurry up and build a travois with what's left of that door, then we can take turns getting him back to my cabin. The storm's still brewing, but I don't think the worst of it's stirred up yet. From those clouds, I'd say we have an hour or two yet."

"Just enough time." Slocum had already anticipated the need for a travois and had dragged the tattered door off the remaining strap hinge. "We get to your cabin, I'll leave you to tend Jigger. He's worse off than he lets on. I'll go try to find our escapee, then head to the Tamarack and roust Frenchy and the boys."

21

"Boy, if you want any amount of respect from me, you'll have to be doing what I want you to do, not what you think would be best." Whitaker pulled on his cigar, then pulsed a blue cloud into his son's face.

The big soft-faced boy just stood there, eyeing his father with a mixture of curiosity and sadness.

"Judging by your expression, I'd guess you don't have a clue what I'm talking about. That right, Jordan?"

The boy stood staring at his father for a moment longer, then said, "That's not strictly true, Papa. I know just what it is you want and what you want me to do about it, but I don't necessarily agree with what it is you want."

"What on earth do you mean by that, boy?" Whitaker struggled to push himself forward in his cantankerous desk chair. "You think you know better than I do how to run my business?"

"No, sir, Papa. But I do know that if you treat people nicely, they are more apt to do the same to you."

"What am I running, a Bible study class? I guess to hell

not!" Whitaker stuffed the cigar into his lips, clawed his hands to the edge of his desk, and yanked himself forward, sputtering and growling hard enough that he bit clean through the cigar. The glowing end fell into his lap and instigated a whole new round of rage.

His son thought that Papa Whitaker sounded and looked a whole lot like a fat, angry chicken.

"Papa, all I'm saying is that I'm beginning to see a whole lot of people in this town who aren't too happy with how things are beginning to turn for them."

"That's not my fault!" said the little fat man.

Jordan backed toward the door. "I think it is, Daddy. It's happened before. Remember Wickenburg? Remember Dalton? Excelsior?"

"Shut up, Jordan. Just shut your fat face. What do you know about it anyway? You were just a boy. You and your mama, always hanging on my coattails, begging for pennies while I did what I had to do to build up a grubstake, get us set up somewhere, then move on to someplace bigger, more promising. That's the only way in life to get anywhere. You know it and I know it."

"No, Papa. No, I don't. Me and Ermaline, now that we're fixing to get married, we figured to talk with you about all this, maybe see if we can't all sit together around the family dining table and . . ." The big boy ran the toe of his brogan along a yellowed crescent pattern on the worn carpet in front of him.

Now, thought Whitaker, this is an interesting turn of events. On the one hand, my dimwit son is telling me how to run my own business, my own self-built empire. On the other hand, he's doing what I've always wanted him to do, to show an interest in something besides whatever it is he's spent his dull life interested in. Hmm. It occurred to Whitaker that he didn't really know much about the boy, other than the fact that they'd had little in common much of the boy's twenty-odd years. Didn't even know rightly how old the boy was. All he knew for certain was that when his wife died, the care and feeding of the oaf had been tossed in his lap. So he'd sent the boy off to school back East, and he had to admit the idea came to him by way of news that Jigger McGee had done the same with his daughter.

Who would have thought that the two of them, one a firebrand like her father, and the other a dullard not at all like his father, would end up back here in the little logging town of Timber Hills, and actually hit it off?

That day had been a blessing in disguise, as far as Whitaker was concerned. It had provided him with the vague but promising buddings of a plan to get hold of Jigger's properties, his influence, his everything. That was one thing he was pleased about, and he had the boy to thank for that, he guessed.

He'd take being saddled with the boy forever at his side—or at least within striking distance—if he could at least have Ermaline as a daughter-in-law. Provided he also got everything the girl's father possessed.

"Now, son," purred a calmer Whitaker, staring at the big red-faced boy before him. "Come on back over here. Have a seat in that chair in front of the desk, and let's do something we've never done before."

Whitaker almost choked on the thing he was about to say, but he plowed on ahead. "Let's discuss this matter like two . . . businessmen. Over a cigar and a sip of whiskey, shall we?"

"I don't drink nor smoke, Papa. You ought to know that."

"Confound it, boy! Set your ass down in that chair and at least make some sort of effort to have a man-to-man discussion with me!" Whitaker felt his face redden, worked to relax his bunched jaw muscles. If this kept up, he'd not have to worry about building up his empire—the boy would do him in, make his heart explode right here and now in this office.

The boy surprised him by sitting down, albeit warily, as if Whitaker might lunge at him any second.

"Good, good. Now, what I want you to do, son, sometime soon, is bring your intended to our humble home for a nice meal. Then we'll all set down around the family table, as you say, and we'll have us a big ol' business meeting."

He watched his big son amble on out the door, pulling on his wool overcoat and cinching his wool scarf up around his head as if he were about to disappear into it altogether. He paused at the door. "Thanks, Papa. See you later."

"Bye, son." Whitaker kept the smile pasted on until the oaf had left his office and the door closed behind him. Then he scowled, let his chewed cigar droop, and rubbed his cold hands together, trying to figure out where the best place to meet up with his future daughter-in-law might be. He had a business proposition for the young thing, and it didn't involve the boy.

22

It took the weary little troupe longer than Slocum had expected to reach Hella's cabin. For the first mile or so she kept offering to help drag the travois, and it finally dawned on him that she was as tough or tougher than most men he'd ever met, had to be to live the life she did, and he'd need all the strength he could muster when he lit out after that fool drunk they'd beaned and left for later.

"Okay, then," Slocum said finally as he slowed his dragging efforts, glad for the break, however brief. "Never let it be said John Slocum didn't give a trapper woman a fair shake."

"Oh, you did that and plenty last night," she said, smiling, "but you're as stubborn as any man I've ever met. Maybe more so."

"There are things a man can't change about himself," he said, shrugging out of the makeshift harness they'd fabricated from ropes scavenged from an old, sagging bed in the cabin.

"Ha! You mean there are things a man won't change about himself."

He shook his head. "You believe what you need to and I'll do the same. The thing I believe most in is getting us all back to your cabin safe and sound."

"Can't argue with that."

He arched an eyebrow her way.

"Don't say a thing, John Slocum." She bent to the task, and with Slocum's help got the travois sliding. As he clomped along beside her, he made sure Jigger was still okay, bundled up and breathing, and then he worked as best he could with his frozen hands and leather chopper mittens to rig up another harness so they might both haul the travois. Soon he was pulling alongside her.

"There now, John Slocum, isn't this better than being bullheaded?" She was nearly shouting now as they trudged uphill into the raking teeth of the storm. They had nearly made it over what he hoped was the last rise before the long ravine that led to her cabin.

He had also hoped that the storm of the night before would mark the end of the pattern, but she had been right when she told him that last night's blow felt to her like a lead-up to a bigger storm. This one drove at them like a constant, battering fist.

Somewhere on the trek back to her cabin, the wind seemed to double in strength with each minute that passed. Soon they could barely see, though it was midday. Slocum was about to comment on it as a way to make sure she was feeling well and not succumbing to the harsh conditions when a guttural howl pierced the freezing, blowing cold.

Almost immediately another sounded, from just across the trail, on the opposite side. They seemed to Slocum to draw closer, or maybe it was the wind playing tricks on him. No, there they were again, definitely closer this time. On both sides of them.

Slocum held an arm out to Hella, drawing her to a stop. She glanced at him, then back through the blowing snow toward the tight trees on both sides of them. She wasn't smiling this time, but neither did she seem concerned.

"They won't harm us. Don't worry."

But Slocum wasn't so easily convinced. Even Hella groaned at the increasingly savage noises. It sounded to Slocum as if someone was tearing something apart and reveling in the very act. "Come on," said Hella and they resumed their labors, lugging the travois. Jigger settled down and seemed to fall asleep again, his head lolling and wobbling with each step they took.

Back at the wrecked cabin, Jigger had been their first priority, so they'd bundled him up and strapped him down, but as the storms whipped up in intensity, Slocum knew they'd made the right decision in leaving that battered place. Before they left, he'd done his best to put out the fire in the stove and barricade the door. He figured someone would want to return to cart off the body, see if there were any other clues as to why the two men had done what they'd done.

He suspected he'd find the answer to that question in the little town of Timber Hills, and probably at the desk of one Torrance Whitaker. He'd ask Hella about it as soon as they got to the cabin, but right now, the storm took all he had to offer breathwise and more just to keep on trudging forward. He noticed that Hella was lagging a little behind, and he compensated with his own tugging, hopefully without her noticing. She was a proud woman—that was for certain.

As if his thoughts had nudged her, Slocum felt the travois give a little lurch. He glanced at her, seeing mostly blinding white pelting snow now, but knowing she was there.

"Almost there!" she shouted at him, and he wondered how the hell she knew where they were. One stinging snow pellet looked like another to him. But sure enough, up ahead he saw a low, dark mass before them. The cabin?

They reached the same low-hung entryway they'd crowded into the night before and made certain that Jigger was pulled up tight to the cabin. Then Slocum bent down to unfasten his snowshoes, but Hella grabbed his shoulder, bent low to his ear. "Something's wrong."

"What?" he said, bending close to Jigger.

"No," she said, holding her face close to his ear and whispering. Even though she was close, he still had trouble hearing her over the snapping wind. "Someone's been here—might still be."

He didn't bother asking her how she knew—it was the same instinct that told her where she was, even in the midst of a whiteout. He merely nodded, stripped off the mitten on his gun hand, then motioned for her to stay with Jigger and keep away from the door. He bent, crabwalking low to the door, tried the latch gingerly, his numb fingers unable to function without him seeing them, willing his mind to force the hand to push upward lightly on the thick-carved spindle.

He was familiar with such mechanisms, and knew this relied on a length of rawhide on the inside. But he also knew it could just as easily be deadbolted with the sliding wood and steel bar he'd seen earlier. Might be that whoever was in there had locked it. In which case he'd have to ask her if there was some other way in. She had windows but had kept them tightly shuttered, he assumed, to keep out the stormy weather.

But with her familiarity with the skoocooms and being a lone person living on her own out here, it might be that she was also interested in keeping the potential for danger at arm's length.

He put an ear to the door but heard nothing more than the wind at his back and maybe his own heart thudding in his chest. He couldn't even detect light leaking out from under doors or shutters. He continued lifting the latch, and so far, smidgen by smidgen, it kept rising. Soon it rose no more, so he kept a light pressure on it, lest the door spring inward and startle whoever might be on the outside looking in.

Wait, there was a sound, barely there, but something. There it was again . . . a sobbing sound? Slocum made sure with a glance that his Colt was still in his hand and the hammer thumbed back—it was so cold he couldn't feel it—and keeping low, he nudged the door open.

It was dark inside, save for the dim glow of a handful of coals in the hearth from their early-morning fire. Hella had banked it well, counting on nursing the remaining coals back to life once they returned with whatever cargo they had been able to bring back. In this case, they had thankfully found Jigger. But the sounds Slocum was hearing weren't coming from any of them on the outside of the door.

Once he nudged the door open and saw by the dimmest of light from the coals, his eyes adjusted while he edged ever deeper into the cabin on his knees, Colt held out straight and true, despite the cold. And soon he was able to make out a vague shape—long and prone—before the fire. It convulsed, jerking and almost thrashing. Just as quickly as it began, it stopped, followed by a long, moaning cry, like too much air being forced through a thin rip in a weak vessel.

It was a man. Slocum got to his feet, and even before he made it to the man's side, he knew who it was. It had to be the man they'd knocked unconscious. "Hella!" Slocum bellowed, but she was already heading in through the door. "Light a lamp, I'll bring Jigger in, then we can get this fire blazing. This man's nearly dead!"

"He's the last person I expected to see here. I thought he'd gone the other way." Hella chattered like a blue jay while she bustled about the cabin, lighting lamps, building up the fire—she had it blazing in seconds. They laid both men out before the fireplace, kept Jigger wrapped tight in a fresh layer of bedding, and as soon as water warmed, Hella doctored his head wounds properly.

The other man was in far worse shape. Once the lamps were glowing, the light revealed that some of his fingers, as well as the one foot that had somewhere, somehow become unbooted, had begun to blacken from the cold. His long-handles were torn and bloody, and furrowed jags cut into his thin, bony body beneath.

They weren't deep cuts but they were numerous, as if his attacker had done this with the intention of slowness and deliberation. His forearms, back, thighs—all looked as if he'd been raked by a she-cat. And his face, which they had both seen but a few hours before, bore the distinct signs of having been battered by repeated blows. His brow had bubbled in a long band of swelling, blood pooling behind. And his nose and one cheekbone looked to have been pounded flat, as if backhanded by some giant brute.

As they tended him, Slocum and Hella both felt not a little guilty over the man's rough treatment.

"Skoocoom do this?" he said.

"I'd guess so, yeah." She nodded. "They're pretty fair judges of good and bad. Got their own way of keeping things even, if you know what I mean."

Slocum slit the man's longhandles and peeled them away from his raw leg. The man, half-conscious, sucked in a harsh breath through blackened lips. "Judge and jury of the woods, huh?" said Slocum.

"You might not like it, and I might have a hard time with their methods sometimes, but you have to admit they're a cut above a grizzly in certain respects."

"I suppose so," he said, wringing out a bloodied rag in a crock of tepid, crimson water.

"They're fond of Jigger, I take it?"

She looked at him. "As a matter of fact, they are. He's

been . . . shall we say . . . kind to them over the years. They don't forget things like that. They also don't take kindly to trash like this"—she jerked her chin at the very man she was in the midst of doctoring—"hurting someone they like."

"I expect they'd do the same for you, then?"

She looked at him fully. "What makes you think I'm friendly with the skoocoom?"

"Just a guess. Otherwise, why would they nearly kill this poor fool, then drag him all the way over here and dump him in your cabin, where they knew you'd find him?"

"Doesn't mean I'm friendly with them."

"Don't mean it don't, neither."

They both jerked their eyes toward Jigger. The old man's eyes were wide open, as wide as his bloodied and bandaged head would allow anyway, and the makings of a smile played on his mouth.

"Jigger! You're back with us!"

"You darn right I am. Didn't think a couple of ol' wood rats could keep me down, did you?"

"Not hardly, no," Hella said.

"Knew I could count on you the moment I met you back on the trail that day, Slocum. You're a good egg, you are." By the time he'd finished speaking, Jigger's color had drained once again from his face and his words slurred, his eyelids fluttered.

"Jigger, stop talking and go to sleep," she said. "I don't need to bring two of you so-called wood rats back from the brink. Hard enough job ahead of us for one—and he wouldn't make a patch on your pants. But a living thing's a living thing."

If Jigger heard her, he didn't let on. He was too busy drifting back into a deep slumber. Soon, a soft whistling sound escaped from his nose.

"Good," she said. "I've about had enough of his chattiness. Work to do." She pushed by Slocum and retrieved another pan from the hearth. The water in it steamed and sloshed as she set it down. "Nearly through with him. I don't have much in the way of medicines here. If time and whiskey can't take care of it, then I figure I'm through anyway. Got a few Indian herbs that might help, though." She rummaged in a cupboard and came up with a small leather pouch cinched tight. "You want to get this steaming in one of those cups?" She tossed the satchel to Slocum. "I'll get more firewood."

He did as she asked and traded places with her once she brought an armload in. "I'd rather fetch wood, if you don't' mind," he said, smiling. "I'm not as much of a hand at doctoring as you are, and I don't want to hear what Jigger would have to say if he knew I gave him too much of a dose of Indian remedies."

He flipped up his sheepskin collar, tugged on his mittens, and headed outside, the wind and driving snow whistling and sluicing every which way. Hella or her father, whoever had built or added onto the cabin, had designed it well. He assumed that the somewhat protected entryway and overhanging porch roof usually did a fine job in cutting down on the most punishing effects of the storm winds from the high country far above.

Today, though, the house's design was barely adequate, as the wind couldn't seem to make up its mind. Slocum rummaged in a stiff-peaked drift, found the spot where she'd pulled stove-length logs mere moments before—already the wind and snow had begun erasing traces of her efforts—and began loading up his arms.

A loud grunting sound erupted just behind him, and he jerked to his left out of reflex. A sharp pain, then a burst of warmth flowered up the side of his head. He felt the logs fall from his hands, saw the side of the cabin spin upward somehow—but that was impossible, wasn't it? Cabins didn't float or fly, did they? Then he saw the gray blanket of stormy sky and swirling snow press down on him from above, felt himself hit the snow behind him. Have I fallen?

More sounds, grunting and growling, but low and close to his ears, filled his brain. Then through the snow and wind he smelled something pungent, raw and rank, worse than a dozen Arizona outhouses baking in a July sun. But raw and all animal, as if he'd just crawled up a grizzly's backside and couldn't find the way out. What was happening? Did a grizz catch him by surprise? And why couldn't he seem to make his arms work? He tried with all his effort to lash out and managed to swing an arm outward. It hit something, he heard a grunt, then whatever was there must have hit him— maybe the same thing had hit him before?

It struck the other side of his head, and he felt the same warm pain, and felt as if a hot, smelly rag were being pulled over his head. Then, as all that gray light above flickered like a guttering flame in a strong breeze, he felt himself moving, being dragged backward.

In his last moment of consciousness, Slocum looked up at the snowy, gray sky and saw a big, big hairy face staring down at him, the homeliest man he'd ever seen. Only this big, ugly man had huge green-yellow eyes.

23

Torrance Whitaker tugged on a newly shined pair of brogans and smoothed the lapels on his best suit coat. He paused a moment and gazed out the window once again. It had proven to be yet another corker of a day, the weather so foul that he could just now, in the early afternoon, barely see a couple of feet into the street.

He sighed, wondering why he hadn't heard from those two fools by now. He realized that they weren't exactly competent, but he'd expected them to at least come back. Guess I'll have to do the job myself . . . somehow, he thought. Whitaker slowly realized that that ignoramus son of his was not up to the task, and never would be. Why had it taken him so long to realize it? Could it be he actually had a soft spot where his own progeny was concerned?

Whitaker snorted. He doubted that very much. More than likely it was that he wanted to see the kid fail. Full-out, fall flat on his face one more time. Maybe for the last time— wouldn't that be enough? One last time, before the entire town, then he could show just how he was so much more effective than anyone else, even his own son.

"Hell, I don't know. I'm no deep thinker anyhow. Just a businessman. A self-made businessman," said Whitaker, giggling a little bit. Maybe from the whiskey he'd taken to fortify himself for the upcoming conversation he had planned. Something about that girl of McGee's made him a little nervous. He didn't mind admitting it—if only to himself.

She was a strong-willed woman. He'd seen the signs of it. Got that from her father, from an early age, no doubt. And that reminded him of his now-dead wife, Jordan's mother. He counted his lucky stars every day that she'd up and died when she did—elsewise she'd be the one calling all the shots, ruling his days and nights and keeping him as her whipping boy.

He stumped on through the saloon, his saloon, as he liked to remind himself every time he set foot in the place or exited, for that matter. How many people did he know who owned saloons? Well, not counting the others in town. But that was a pretty low number compared with the number of folks who sought refreshment or enjoyment through those doors.

And then out he went into the cold, snowy afternoon. As he buttoned his wool coat's collar high against the bracing, biting wind, he thought that before too many more years passed, he might just up and sell his holdings hereabouts and take a big ol' carpetbag filled with money on southward toward warmer weather.

Or, he thought, I might be better off to retain all ownership of my holdings myself and hire someone, say someone just like Ermaline McGee—his future daughter-in-law—for instance.

That thought ferried him all the way down to the boardinghouse where she currently resided. And just as if she was expecting him, Ermaline herself opened that door and smiled. "Mr. Whitaker, or should I say . . . Daddy-to-be?"

She flashed him a wicked grin and beckoned him on into the sitting room. Before he could even say howdy or boo, she closed the door and started right in. "Now what's all this I hear from Jordan? He says you want a meeting with us? Something about how you wanted to talk with little old me?"

"Well now," said Whitaker, shrugging out of his coat. "That's just about the size of it, yes, it is. Sure thing. Only let me get situated, will you?"

But she didn't. She lit right into him, in the most appealing tones, and even as he knew he was being manipulated, Whitaker couldn't help appreciating her keen edge. She was a human skinning knife, and if he didn't use care, that little she-devil might just peel him clean, hide, hair, meat, and bone.

"Now hold, hold I say, little girl."

And she finally did. But it chafed her, he knew, and even that he appreciated. She would be the very one to help him carry off this plan. A little tension in the business—that was what he needed to buy up all the rest of the region and make it his kingdom, fit for himself to rule.

What does she want out of it, though? For surely a woman such as this, he thought, with such business savviness, knows what she seeks, and surely she wants something. A cut of the take? She might just assume she was getting that once she married his son. Well, she would be surprised if she thought that she would inherit it all, wouldn't she? How did all that work anyway?

As the meeting wore on, it became clear to Whitaker that his fears—or suspicions—about her were correct. She was a smart young thing, maybe too smart. But hadn't he thought the same? And she was bold, too, in her plans. He could tell she felt something for his son, so maybe she wasn't wholly rapacious. Though he suspected she was . . .

And she wanted her father taken care of. Who could blame her? But that was the point where the whole thing sort of fell apart. There was no way he was going to let her know that he'd tried—and in all likelihood failed, since he hadn't heard a thing from those two imbeciles he'd hired—to have her father removed from the running, as he liked to consider it.

Sometime later, as he tugged on his wool overcoat and was ushered to the front door, he told himself that there was no way he was going to be bowled over by her. And yet as he roamed on homeward, he had to stop several times in the street to recount bits and pieces of their conversation. Had he really agreed to that? And the other point she raised? Oh dear oh dear, he thought. I best keep my wits about me around this little girl . . .

Later, when Torrance Whitaker finally laid his head down on his pillow and snuggled tight under the layers of quilts, he didn't once consider his lumpy son's feelings. Rather, he thought about all that she had proposed—and how very much of it matched perfectly, as if bookended, with his thinking, his plans and schemes and dreams for this odd, unlikely, but promising little mountain town that timber built.

"Oh," he had told her. "There is no doubt that your father, Jigger McGee, was the founder of Timber Hills. No one else can lay claim to that title."

Snuggled deep under the covers in his bed, he recalled her earnest young face nodding in full agreement with him, yes, yes, she'd all but said. Daddy Jigger's a good, good man.

"But," Whitaker had been careful to say, "there comes a time in every town's life when it must grow, or wither and die on the vine." He'd been sure to give her a long, slow nod then, to be sure she'd gotten the emphasis of what he'd just said. And yes, she was a smart girl, no doubt, and she had understood him. And with that last recalled thought in mind, Torrance Whitaker drifted off to sleep, a smile on his face.

*

24

Slocum awoke not with a start, but with a slow overall full-body numbness that seeped into him, with the measured pace of an oozing mudslide. What was happening to him? He worked hard to force his eyes open, and when he felt he'd finally succeeded, he still couldn't see anything. Then it occurred to him that maybe he was in the dark, pitch black. He worked to raise his arms, but they felt pinned somehow.

What had happened? He urged himself to think. Think harder—something had hit him. Where? When? At Hella's cabin, that was the last place he remembered being. He had been helping her to doctor Jigger and the other man, then . . . then . . . he went for more firewood! And something happened outside, something about hot pain, a . . . hideous face staring at him. Hairy . . .

The skoocoom? Couldn't be—he still didn't much believe the stories, even if he'd been confronted with plenty of tall tales about it, been told it existed from otherwise sane-seeming men and women, had heard animal noises he'd never quite heard before from creatures of the night.

He'd heard all manner of big beast—grizzlies, mountain lions, wolves, hell, even the ravings of hydrophobic men— and yet nothing had quite sounded like that strange howling, guttural cry, as if whatever had made it had been in pain and wanted to tell the world about it.

Despite all that, Slocum was hesitant to believe that the thing that had dry-gulched him outside the cabin had been anything but a man. And then another quick snippet of memory pierced his throbbing mind: There was a face, a horrible face with those raw green eyes. And that face with those vicious eyes had been covered in hair. How do you explain that, Mr. Know-It-All? he asked himself.

He ran that question in his mind, chewing on it like a bite of tough steak, and he came to the sudden judgment that though he didn't have an answer, there had to be one that didn't involve tales of a hair-covered giant man and his weird brood stomping through the forests hereabouts.

All these thoughts ran through his mind in the time it took to pull in a few long breaths, breaths that came hard because he was somehow bound so tightly. At least he thought he was bound. He couldn't lift his arms, legs, head. Hell, he wasn't even sure his eyes were open. And then something occurred to him—smells. It was as if someone had unstoppered his nose and ears.

The smells came first—raw, violent, nostril-twitching smells that raked his senses like a bull grizzly's breath after he'd fed on a long-dead, maggot-crawling deer corpse. But there was more to it, as well. More than animal. It smelled almost human in its origin. Somehow it was as if ten hard-working cowhands on a long, hot trail drive had decided to sit close to a woodstove in a small line shack, and then strip off their socks and drape them to sizzle and sputter and steam on the stove top.

And running through that, the pungent, gagging stink of someone with a severe gut ailment who had just devoured a potful of frijoles, then released all that stink in the only way men knew how.

And the smells were followed closely by sounds, low rumbling . . . snores? But they were more than that—they were choking, rasping snores as if emitted by giant men with massive bellows-like chests, a series of them, too many to count to find out how many men there might be, sawing wood in the dark. And then came the farting noises, long wet streams that strove to match the stink he already smelled.

And that was when Slocum gagged and fought for air and tried with all his ability to raise his arms to his mouth, to his nose, out of reflex, for fear of vomiting on himself and choking to death. His own throaty, wet-snot sounds, of a sudden, halted some of the other sounds, some of the snoring. And they were soon replaced with grunts, then the grunts were replaced with angry, sneering sounds, no words, just angry, dark, growling sounds.

Oh Lord, thought Slocum, what in the holy hell is that?

25

"Near as I can figure, them two was hired by Whitaker to do me in." Jigger grunted as he scooched higher up to a sitting position. "I tried to listen but they conked me on the bean good and hard before I could get much deciphering in. Ain't that just the way, though."

"What's he got against you, Jigger?" Hella said, tucking in the covers around him.

"Oh, stop mother-henning me, girl. We got to go after Slocum!"

She scowled at him. "I know all about that, and I'm about to light out—but not you, you're too weak. Besides, someone has to keep an eye on the prisoner."

"You mean that half-dead rascal with the black feet and busted-up face?" Jigger cracked a smile. "He ain't going nowhere."

"That's right, he's not," she said. "Because you're going to be here to make sure he stays put. Now answer my question, McGee—what's Whitaker got against you?"

Jigger's face grew hot, but he finally relented—she had

helped to save his life, after all. "Now listen, Miss Bossy, just because your daddy and me was friends don't give you the right to be all—"

"Bossy?" she said, smiling.

"You know, you ain't changed much since you was a kid."

"Same goes for you, I'd imagine. Now, are you going to answer my question? I'm asking because, like it or not, I'm involved now. And as you're my oldest friend, I think I deserve to know what I'm up against."

"Oh, all right then." Jigger rasped a callused old hand over his beard. "That bastard isn't satisfied with owning half the town. He wants it all—and he wants the rest of my land, too. Plus, he wants the bank—he's made himself top dog of that outfit, too, you know."

"No, I didn't know that. Good thing I don't have any money," she said. "Even if I did, I don't think I'd put it in a bank. Why would anyone do such a thing anyway?"

If Jigger had heard her, he didn't let on. He was on a roll and wasn't about to let someone else's comments interrupt his own. "And!" He raised a bony finger as if he were testing the wind. "He's got my daughter!"

That halted her as she tugged on her well-worn wool-and-fur mackinaw. "What do you mean?"

"I mean Ermaline is all set to become his . . . daughter-in-law. Can you imagine?"

The very words he spoke seemed to drain the blood from Jigger's face. It looked to Hella as if he had aged ten years right before her eyes.

"She wants to marry Jordan?" Hella couldn't quite bring herself to say it with a straight face.

"Go ahead and laugh," said Jigger. "I about did—then I got to thinking about it and wondered how on earth anyone who come from my loins could willingly hook themselves up with such a family. So I confronted her."

"You didn't," said Hella.

"Did so."

"And what did she say?"

"Said she was in love with that big fool boy. Can you imagine? I doubt it very much. In fact, I think she's been hypnotized or some such by that fat bastard Whitaker. But what can you do?"

Hella hoisted her pack basket on her back, hefted her rifle, and headed for the door. "Love is a powerful thing, Jigger. Like as not, she was blindsided by the fact that she fell in love with him, too. Especially knowing as I do how much such a union would drive you around the bend."

"You ain't half wrong, girly. But I ain't there yet. If I have anything to say about it, they won't never be wed. Hell, I had my way, I'd make sure Jordan was run out of town on a pole, tar and feathers his only company. Same goes double for his foul father."

Hella shook her head as she opened the cabin door. "Keep an eye on that one there, Jigger. I'll be back as soon as I can. I have a feeling I know what happened to Mr. Slocum, but I won't know for sure for a while yet. That shotgun's at hand and loaded, and there's plenty of stew and coffee on the hearth. You sure you can get over there okay?"

"Girly, you keep on mother-henning me and I will fly out of this bed and chase you down in the snow. Now go on and find Slocum!"

She did, and the last thing she heard as she slammed the door was Jigger's cackle, halfway between a laugh and a cough. He still wasn't right, although he'd never been what you could call a normal person. But then again, thought Hella, who in the heck was she to claim to know what was normal or not? She was a single woman living out in the mountains, alone, and trapping and skinning animals for a living.

She chuckled as she swung down the easy-to-follow trail left by Slocum's abductors. She was not afraid of them in the least, just curious to know why they felt the need to abscond with him.

Then she knew—they were worried about her, protective of her. That had to be it. But Slocum? He seemed perfectly harmless, had helped her. Oh dear, she thought, maybe one of them is jealous? Wouldn't that be something? The oddness of the entire situation made her feel warm inside, as well as a little strange. And the more she dwelt on the odd topic, the more uncomfortable she became—and the more worried she grew. What if Slocum was in danger? She really hadn't thought that would be the case, but . . . what if?

Even though she knew that John Slocum was as self-reliant as any man she'd ever met, and quite capable of more than she knew, the thought that he might be in danger forced her into a faster lope along the trail she suspected was the right one, sudden fear beginning to gnaw her from the inside out.

Slocum knew his eyes were open now, as that strange yellow-green glow from those big, angry eyes pierced the stinking, pitch-black gloom. His head throbbed and hummed like a sack of angry bees. Whatever had clobbered him on the noggin had really done a trick on him—he hoped his ears would stop ringing, even though he could certainly hear all the damnable noises of his captors.

But his own ills, aches, and pains were the least of his concerns right now. He had to make darn sure whatever this thing was didn't kill him. But how to do that when he couldn't move his limbs? And as he struggled, he watched the bright eyes blink closed, heard the muffled shufflings of what had to be huge feet drawing closer.

Hell, everything about this . . . thing . . . seemed huge.

And when the eyes opened again, the thing was directly above him, those eyes staring down at him, the stink of its breath descending, drawing closer, the sound of its breathing—a chuffing, rasping grunt—along with it.

I have never been more helpless, Slocum thought. Never. And yet he struggled with every ounce of his fiber and being to raise an arm, kick a leg, clench a fist—anything. But nothing worked. He tried to shout, and that, too, failed him. At least I can breathe, he told himself, until whatever this thing was, and it sure seemed bent on destroying him, did whatever it intended to do.

Then something whooshed through the air and struck him hard in the right side. He felt himself pitch to the opposite side, but snap right back. Something kept him pinned, but it also had moved—whatever it was that pinned his right arm and leg had moved! He worked harder to move those limbs and damned if he didn't feel something giving way, even just a little bit. Yes, now he was certain of it.

But he wasn't able to move fast enough to dodge the next blow. As with the first one, the punch was accompanied by a grunting bark, short and clipped, as if issued to emphasize the blow. It rocked him to the left once again, but this time Slocum was prepared for it—as well as he could be anyway. He did his best to rock with it, jerking hard on his left arm, and something else gave way. His arm popped free of the weight that had been placed on it, and he arched the arm with all the strength he could muster. It ranged upward, sloppily, almost lazily, but then it hit something.

Though it was buzzing with pins and needles, his hand felt that whatever it hit was hard and hairy. He tried to scrabble for a handhold in it, but his arm flopped back down again. He gritted his teeth and brought it back up. This time it hurt like hell but at least he could feel it, and that, he knew, was a good thing. He lowered it, then a sudden thought occurred to him—he might still be armed, might still have his weapons. Now that one hand was free, he'd perhaps be able to search for them.

Even though he couldn't see in the dark, that didn't mean that whatever creature this was couldn't—he was convinced it could. But he could still feel with that free hand. And he crabbed it down to his waist, along the right side, as fast as he was able.

And though the pins and needles were still making themselves painfully felt, there was something of substance beneath his roving fingertips now. Whatever he'd hit—and that had hit him—didn't react, oddly enough. At least not yet. He suspected he'd get clouted again any second. So he took advantage of the opportunity to find a weapon, a rock, anything.

He was rewarded with the telltale feeling of the hilt of his big skinning knife beneath his throbbing fingertips. He picked with frantic fingers at the rawhide thong securing it in place. Too late!

Slam came another blow. Slocum kept his hand gripped tightly to the handle of the still-sheathed knife, but stiffened and worked hard to roll with the blow. He felt his leg jerk free of whatever it was that had pinned him. He was beginning to suspect it was a log, maybe a rock or two, though he wasn't entirely convinced. And he didn't really much care. He just wanted to be armed and ready to gut whatever this damn thing was that insisted on causing him such misery.

Come on! He urged his fingertips to unlace the thong, and was finally rewarded with a loosening of the tie-downs. A little more, little more . . . and the grunting sound came again, just before the next clout. This time, however, the blow came from the left side. Good, thought Slocum. Now I can get my other arm out of prison.

The more clouts he received, even as he worked to free

the knife and use it to whatever end he might be forced to, Slocum became convinced that his captor was playing with him. Not unlike a grizzly before a kill—or after. But this thing had to know he was alive. He'd just hit it, after all. And done his best to thrash and try to free himself.

26

"There ain't a thing I can't handle, you little rascal. So keep all that in mind when you decide to surprise me and leap to your feet. You know as well as I do you ain't got a snowball's chance in Hades, but I tell you what . . ." Jigger knew he was talking to a half-dead man, but it did him good to be able to address as he saw fit—as he wanted to—one of the men who'd nearly snuffed out his living days. He didn't care if the man would in all likelihood not live out the week, let alone walk again on that blackened gimpy pin of his. Frostbite was a hard taskmaster. But the man had brought it on himself.

Still, as many times as Jigger had seen bad cases of it— bad enough that men lost fingers, ears, noses, feet, hands, and sometimes their lives—he tried to keep concentrating on the fact that the man was a rascal. No less deserving of Slocum's gun-blazing wrath that had laid his foul partner low. But somehow he'd lived. That had to count for something.

"Hey, you . . . mister." Jigger had hobbled over to the man's side on the length of fluffed blankets before the fire

Hella had arranged for him. "I say, fella . . ." Still no response.

He leaned close, heard the man's thready, rasping voice. Still alive, still breathing, still as slow and labored as two minutes before when he had checked on him. "Dammit all to hell, fella. By all rights I should kick you out in the snow, let nature finish you off and take you as one of her own, let some mangy critter drag you off as a piss-poor meal. But . . ."

So what's the problem, Jigger? he asked himself. Has age softened your brain, made you a weak little sister? He scratched his chin. Must be, he thought, elsewise how on earth would he sit here in this same room with a man who had done all he could to profit from kidnapping him, then admitted if his plan had come to happen, he and his partner were going to kill him off anyway? Oh boy, oh boy. I have gone soft, thought Jigger.

Because the old Jigger, the real one who chewed wire and spit nails for breakfast each day, would have gotten his pins under him as fast as possible and then gone on down to Timber Hills to deal with Whitaker once and for all.

The very thought, which hadn't occurred to Jigger since his rescue, that Whitaker was at that moment running around, miles below in town, while Jigger was holed up in the mountains, made Jigger instantly enraged. He still felt like a warmed-over gut pile, but at least he could see almost straight now. And he could walk.

"And if I can walk," he said to the near-dead man laid out before the fire, "then I can by gum get myself down to that little town and take away from Whitaker what he drove you and your worthless pal to try to take away from me."

He shook a pointing finger at the prone man. "Don't you think I'm giving up on you. I'll do what I have to do, then I'll be back. If you're dead by then, me and Slocum'll give you a decent burial—which is more than you deserve for what you did to me. But if your hide is still warm, I'll tote you down myself on a sled to Timber Hills, wait for the territorial judge to hang you from the highest tree around. Until then . . ." He turned away, looking for gear to gather for the sudden journey he was about to make. "Until then, mister, you take care. Stay warm—and alive, you hear?" He cackled, then said, "You owe me that much, seeing as how your partner robbed me of my rightful justice. Now, where are my boots?"

It didn't take Jigger but ten minutes, even at his ailment-slowed pace, to gather up the necessary gear to head out into the dwindling storm. He figured he had as much chance as anybody in these woods. They were his, after all. Spiritually if not on a deed. Some of them, yes, but other hunks of acreage, not any longer. Still, he had enough land holdings in his purse to make him a significant threat to Whitaker.

As he finished slowly lashing on the second snowshoe, he pulled in a deep draught of bracing air. Still-falling snow pellets stung his cheeks, sneaked up his nose, felt like hot needle tips. The air felt good inside and out, but he hated to admit that it hurt, too. He'd had broken ribs in the past, so he knew the best method of letting them knit back together was time and little exertion. And he had room in his life for indulging in either. He had to make fast time, get to town. And put his shotgun to good use.

27

As soon as his right leg popped free from under what he was sure was a log, Slocum heaved himself with all the strength he could muster and rolled leftward. He'd regained enough sensation in his arm and hand that he felt the hard, knobby surface of the thing that held down his left side. It *was* a log—he felt the bark. And it was at least eight to ten inches around. No wonder the blood flow had been cut off to his limbs. Whatever had put it in place must be a brute. But that much he already knew. Trick was he had to get away from the brute. But he was in the dark, in this thing's den, and half his body wasn't responding.

Another clout and an accompanying growl sent him sprawling. When he piled up against what felt like a cold stone wall, Slocum immediately grabbed for his knife, felt it still there in its sheath, and lifted it free. He might still be in the dark—in more ways than one—but that didn't mean he was going to be toothless. He backed up against the stone, felt like it might be a cave wall, and worked to get himself into an upright position. He drew his legs up close, thinking he might be able to stand up easier from such a position, perhaps by using the stone wall to push against.

He still couldn't see a lick in front of him, but he held the knife with the blade thrust outward, weaving it back and forth in the dark as a snake does its tail, poised, playing, ready to strike should necessity prompt it.

Suddenly from his left came a mighty barking roar, close by, as if he'd accidentally clunked someone. And for all he knew, he may well have—he still had little feeling in his legs.

The sudden growl seemed to elicit others, as if they had all begun to wake up. Slocum had no way of knowing if it was day or night, but knowing what little he did about these so-called skoocooms, it seemed they spent much of their wakeful time roaming the countryside at night. If they were all sleeping now, it was possibly still daytime, and all this ruckus was rousting them before their time. Maybe he'd have an advantage if he could get out of there and hit the trail in the daylight.

He had no idea if any of this made sense. His head was throbbing, and his hands and feet felt as if they were afire. Another clout to his side came out of nowhere. He reacted swiftly, lashing out with the knife. He brought it down in a clumsy swinging arc, slashing and hoping it found purchase somehow in something. And it did.

The howl of pain tinged with rage was as delicious as it was deafening. Beneath the blade, Slocum felt wetness matting into hair. Blood that he had drawn? He certainly hoped so. He worked to keep his blade edges honed enough so that he could shave with them.

He knew this wounded creature was on his right side, had heard others waking up and sounding pretty grumpy to his left. And he knew, too, that he had rolled to this spot from directly in front of him, but beyond that, he had no idea what was in this place.

Sitting in one spot has never gotten you a thing, Slocum, he told himself. And at that moment, when his limbs were barely able to function, when they felt as if they had been dipped in kerosene and set alight, he felt fur brush against his face, something else swat his legs, another something— was it a paw? a hand?—snap at his head, sending it jerking to one side, a mere tap but the power behind it was great, that much he could feel.

And all along, the din of growls and barking, savage noises, of low chuffing sounds, mingling with the stink of these critters, increased in sound and intensity until he felt as if he could take no more.

"Now or never," he muttered, not hearing his own words, barely able to keep from gagging as he took in shallow breaths, expelled them quickly, all through his mouth.

Slocum pushed himself forward onto his knees, knife still clutched tight in his fist so that he might make outward slashing moves or downward jabs. His left arm collapsed with his feeble efforts. He righted himself and kept going. If these creatures could see in the dark, why weren't they attacking? What were they doing? Playing with him? To what end?

He considered it a small gift of time, and took full advantage of it. All around him the sounds grew louder, the smells nastier, but though he sensed great warmth exuding from bulky bodies not far from him to the front, back, sides, he never ran into anything the entire time he scrambled forward. He wanted to stand upright, but he doubted his legs could support him just yet.

Another clout, then another. And rising from the midst of the grotesque sounds all around him, Slocum swore he heard something like . . . chuckling? Nah. Not even possible.

Another swat sent him sprawling sideways. He got up, the chuckling sounds increased—he was without doubt now that it was definitely a laugh-like noise—and something else pushed him from behind, sending him scuttling forward, his hands and knees barely able to keep him from falling. He nearly pitched face-first to the smooth-worn floor, when just before him he saw a dimness in the dark.

At first he kept clambering forward, expecting more punches and swats, but none came. Then he reminded himself that they were, after all, only playing with him. Had to be. That would account for the fact that they hadn't killed him when they plainly could have—or tried to. And it would also account for the fact that he had been hearing a steady and rising chorus of what he could only describe as chuckles and laughter.

Let them laugh, he thought. He didn't care. All he wanted was to get the hell out of there. And the dim glow that he'd seen was the one and only thing he headed for. He felt another seemingly halfhearted swat, then nothing else as he crawled forward, the dim glow becoming brighter with each shambling lunge he took.

Closer and closer to the light, which grew brighter and brighter the closer he drew. And then he smelled fresh air and felt it waft over him—at least it was fresher than what he'd been subjected to inside. And all of a sudden he was out, sliding into low drifts of snow, blue-white in what proved to be afternoon light. The path down which he slid and stumbled and tumbled looked well used, but was hardly in a straight line, winding as it did through snagging trees. Finally, he looked upslope behind him in the dimming day. He spun fully, squared off, and waved his knife with menace before him. He saw nothing.

No huge creatures slamming down the hillside toward him, nothing like it. If he didn't have the sore head and sides and arms and legs to prove it, didn't have the nose that still felt packed with the godawful stink of that dark, dank, cave-like place, he might not believe he'd had the experience at all. But he had.

"John Slocum!"

He turned to see the source of the shouting, downslope from him and working her way up. Hella, the wild mountain woman, hustled upward on her snowshoes, clouds of light snow rising from behind each shoe as she approached.

"You're alive," she said, smiling at him with what looked like genuine relief. It made him feel good.

They both looked at each other a moment. It felt to him as if each knew what the other was thinking. Finally, he said, "Friends of yours, I take it," jerking his head upslope.

She nodded. "They pinned you, eh?"

"How did you know?" he said, rubbing his arms, bending to rub his legs.

"It's what they do."

"To what . . . or who?"

"To whoever or whatever they plan on scaring—"

"Or eating?" said Slocum, straightening and sheathing his knife.

She nodded. "Yes, I'm quite sure a bear could eat a man if he were—"

"A bear? I thought for certain you were going to tell me it was skoocooms."

She snorted, her hands on her hips. "Skoocooms? Do you seriously think, John Slocum, that there are a bunch of overly hairy people running around the woods with no clothes who live in caves without any source of fire for cooking or warmth?"

What Hella said may have been comical sounding, but the way she said it told Slocum he had crossed some sort of thin line with her, one over which she wasn't about to argue. Or maybe she was pulling his leg again. At this point he didn't much care.

"I only meant that it's pretty unlikely, you have to admit," she said.

"Yep," he said.

They walked downhill in silence.

"You left Jigger alone at your cottage?"

"Not alone—he's in charge of the frostbitten bastard."

"I'm surprised you'd leave him there. Ten to one he's gone when we get back."

"What do you mean?"

"He's one ticked-off little man. If you were in his boots, what would you do?" Slocum watched her face in the low light of the trail. Slow realization dawned on her pretty features, and her eyebrows rose. Slocum nodded.

"Whitaker's a dead man if we don't get there in time," said Hella.

"Yep."

"Not such a bad thing."

"Nope. But not something we should let happen, if only because Jigger deserves better than to swing for killing that man."

"Especially out of anger," she said. "And probably no proof that Whitaker was behind any of the kidnapping stuff."

"At least his wounds will slow him down," said Slocum.

She looked at him, then sped up as she neared the dim shape of the cabin. "Don't count on it. There's never been a man as tough as Jigger, you mark my words."

Far behind them on the rough trail they had just punched from on high all the way down to Hella's cabin, a large, hulking shape peered from the trees. It advanced as they did, then stood still when it sensed they might stop and turn.

It had to be certain that the man was not harming her, had to be certain that she cared for the man. And so it had dragged the man off and waited for her to come for him. And she had.

But it was still unsure of something, and so it would follow them to make sure nothing harmed her, the one who had always lived alone in her log cave.

28

"By God, by God, you'd think with all the critters roaming around these parts that I could at least rassle me a bear or a moose or buck or something, heck anything, to get to town even faster." Jigger was feeling pretty good, despite the fact that he was still seeing double. Only time that ever happened for such a long spurt was when he'd been on a toot.

But he reckoned that would clear up before long. Hell, he didn't care one way or another. So long as he could find Whitaker. And if he saw two of him, why, he'd just have to gut 'em both.

As he trudged toward town, the raw cold and creeping snow seemed to find its way under every ragtag piece of clothing he wore. He'd swaddled himself as best he could with bits of his own togs, plus whatever he could find in Hella's cabin. But it didn't seem enough.

"Have to work harder at it, that's all. Make the most of the journey." He grunted with his renewed efforts, stomping faster in the snowshoes. Would he ever get there? "Bah!" he shouted into the blowing snow. Of course he would! It was the blows to his head that put the doubt into him. Normally he was fearless, as sure of himself as nature was that snow would fall and then summer would bring sun.

Soon, though, he tired once again. Felt fatigue weighing him down like a sopping, cold wool blanket. He wasn't certain how long he'd been walking, but he knew his head throbbed and pounded worse than ever, and his legs felt as though they were lengths of sappy green wood. He had nearly reached the big roadside boulder that he knew marked the halfway point, so that told him he had been walking toward Timber Hills for several hours.

By then it was nearly dark, and he felt as though he'd been trudging along for days, with nothing to show for it save a whole lot of aching muscles, a powerful thirst, and a pounding noggin. He leaned against the ice-slick side of the boulder and closed his eyes. He slowly leaned his head back against the mammoth rock and let his confused feelings out in a long, low sigh.

Could be he wasn't in his right mind just yet. Could be Hella knew of what she spoke. Could be he needed to heal up a mite before he lit out after Whitaker. He sighed again and tried to work up the courage to push off the rock and once more take to the trail.

But the very thought of Whitaker's name was enough to force him to grit his teeth, and just at the moment he knew to push himself upright again, he heard a familiar sound, uptrail, but approaching fast. What was it?

No, couldn't be . . . The boys? His boys? Titus and Balzac? No other horses he knew sounded so bold in the snow. Their huffing and blowing, those steady hoofbeats drum-drum-drumming, all taken together made him sure he was hearing his boys, all right. But who would be driving them?

As if in response, he saw his boys picking them up and putting them down, followed tight behind by his old log sledge leaning with the bend of the trail, creaking with the effort, and laden, he could see in the near dark, not by logs, but by men, lots of men. His loggers! One of them near the front held a storm lantern by the bail, swinging it in slow, wide arcs. Another man called out something into the blowing snow.

Jigger raised his arms and was ready to shout when he heard what it was the men were shouting. It was his name, over and over again. "Jigger, Jigger, Jigger . . . "

They nearly coursed by him, so hard were they sliding, but he waved his arms and shouted back, even though the effort felt as though his head were splitting open anew. But it had worked. The man teaming his boys yanked hard on the lines, and the huffing team slowly drummed to a halt a good many sledge lengths past him. Jigger did his best to run toward them. He passed right by the sledge full of men and hugged his boys, Balzac and Titus.

Within seconds, the men had piled off the sledge and were shouting, "Can it be? Jigger? It is, by God!"

They swarmed him, hugging and clapping his back with big, mittened hands. "Where you been? What happened to you?"

All their questions matched his own, and it took a few minutes for each side to get the basic story out of the other. Finally they dragged Jigger aboard the sledge, dosed him liberally with blankets and whiskey, and began singing chorus after chorus of old log camp ditties not fit for any ears other than those of logging men.

And they continued on toward town to help Jigger do what he'd set out to do—and what they also had set out to do: deal with the one man they all agreed was the vicious rascal who deserved nothing but the hard and harsh treatment they would soon see fit to dole out.

29

"Look here," said Hella, bending down, stripping off a mitten and palming barely covered tracks in the narrow mountain logging road.

Slocum thumbed a match alight and lit a small candle stub. The wind had died down to the point where the flames barely guttered. Slocum didn't trust the wind, and just knew it wouldn't be long before another gust whipped up the fresh snow into a rough biting breeze once again. He held a cupped hand close to the flame and bent low to the trail.

"Jigger?"

"Has to be. But look, other tracks. Men's boots, but no snowshoes. And hoofprints." She moved backward on her knees up the trail, feeling with her hand, peering low.

Slocum stayed close, holding the light-giving candle. "Sledge runner," he said. "Lots of men's tracks. Had to be the men from the Tamarack, likely out looking for Jigger."

"And you," she said, looking at Slocum mere inches away.

"Sure," he said, not convinced. Still, it was nice of her to say so. It had been a damn long time since anyone had cared enough about him to send out a gang of men looking for him. It felt good to be included in such sentiment.

"Now what?" said Hella, standing and stretching her back.

"Now," said Slocum, doing the same. "Now we head to town to do the same thing they're likely doing."

"What's that?"

"Track Whitaker. We have to get there in time to prevent a killing. And that's not the worst news."

"It's not?" said Hella.

"Nope. We're on snowshoes."

"Good thing it's all downhill!" She took off at a run, trailing a laugh.

Slocum sighed and put a hand to his sore ribs. As he took off after her, he wondered once again—and not for the last time—what in the hell he was doing up here with all these crazy critters in the mountains anyway.

30

By the time Jigger and his men slid on down the main street of Timber Hills, they were all seeing double, but Jigger was feeling better, he figured, than a man in his condition had any right to feel.

"Girly! Where's my Ermaline at?" Jigger roved up and down the street with his men, bottles in hand, looking for his daughter. "Now split up. And if any of you find my daughter or that weak-kneed soft boy, Jordan, you bring them to me. You hear?"

Old Amos from the livery joined Bumpy from the mercantile—two of Jigger's oldest friends—and tried to persuade him to leave off the foolishness and come with them for a nice big feed at the pancake house. But it didn't work that way. The little logging boss was in high dudgeon, and he had his men with him. There was to be no stopping Jigger McGee that day.

"Whitaker! You come on out here in the street!" Jigger shouted and wobbled on his feet. "I aim to drop you like the sack of bear turds you are!"

Finally Amos and Bumpy did the only thing they knew to do—they fetched Ermaline McGee. She was at least as tough as her old man, might be she could simmer him down. She had been pulling on her boots in the foyer of Mrs. Tigg's boardinghouse when they knocked.

"Course I heard him. I'm not deaf. I was just about to head to the source of all that noise when you two knocked. Now out of my way!" And off she strode, the two older men in her wake, each wondering what levels of excitement the next few minutes might bring to Timber Hills.

"There you are, daughter!" Jigger's voice, a slurred thing from all the whiskey he'd consumed, nonetheless rang up and down the main street. "I been expecting you. Got any more bad news for me?"

"What happened to you, Daddy?"

"Oh, so now you care about what happened to old Jigger, eh?" He took another swig from the bottle he was holding. "Your foul father-in-law-to-be is what happened to me, that's what!"

Daughter or no, Ermaline knew better than to try to take that bottle of spirits away from her father. Once Jigger McGee started drinking, you'd do best to let him finish on his own. Or prepare to draw back a bloody stump.

"Where's that soft bastard you aim to marry anyway?"

"He's probably at home right where he should be. Where anyone with a lick of sense would be if you and your foolish liquored-up log monkeys weren't here disrupting the lives of decent folk."

"Oh, decent folk, is it? Pardon me all to hell." *Glug, glug.* "I thought this here was Timber Hills, the town that Jigger's log monkeys built!"

At that moment, Slocum and Hella trudged into town, bone-tired from pushing so hard to get there on snowshoes. The first thing they saw was the cold main street of the little town beginning to fill with people, half of them loggers from the Tamarack Camp. Rising up from the center, they heard Jigger's rooster-like cackle, matched by a female version of it.

"Maybe we're not too late to save Whitaker's mangy hide," said Hella.

"More to the point, we'd be saving Jigger's skinny neck from a rope," said Slocum, unbuttoning his coat. Though the situation seemed an easy one to defuse, much of it comical, even, given the laughter and drunken wobblings of half the people present, he knew that those very attributes could also cause it to turn on its head with fingersnap speed.

"Hella, you try to find Whitaker. Keep him safe somehow. I'll deal with this lot."

"How are you going to do that?"

"Lady," said Slocum, "I just handled a cave full of skoocooms. Don't you think I can deal with a few drunk loggers?"

"Ha!" she said, heading for the Bluebird Saloon and Whitaker's office. "And I never said they were skoocooms."

"I like that you can lie to me and laugh about it!" He smiled at her retreating form, then shucked his Colt revolver and headed into the crowd.

It didn't take but a few seconds to reach the core—Jigger and his daughter. Had to be her. They bore similar facial features, and Slocum was pleased to see at least she wasn't sporting a beard. Other than that, and her long hair and dress, you could easily match them up as father and daughter.

She was also bossy. And appeared to have command of the situation, because Jigger couldn't get a word in edgewise. The rest of the gathered people, loggers and townsfolk alike, all stood close by, listening to her. "And another thing. I intend to marry Jordan Whitaker, with or without your blessing. I love him, Daddy, and that's all there is to it. I don't know a person in this town who could say he's at all like his father."

"But it's Whitaker's son!" said Jigger in a desperate quick plea.

"And that makes no never mind to me. He's a good man. A bit . . . soft, I will admit. But he's not at all like his daddy."

Jigger let his bottle drop to the hard-packed snow of the street, seemingly defeated. "My Tamarack . . . " he muttered.

"Your Tamarack will be just fine, I promise. Why do you think I have been all nicey-nice with Daddy Whitaker? He is in a good situation right now, but he's not as smart as he thinks. Jordan and I, we both got educated back East and we will be running his affairs soon, and yours, too, if you'll listen to reason and let us. This whole town will be happier and richer than ever, and you won't have all the headaches that have dogged you for years. Don't you see, Daddy? I have strung Whitaker along for you, done all this for you!"

Before Jigger could quite lift his battered head and stare at his daughter with watery, twitchy eyes, the assemblage all threw up their hands and cheered. And then a gunshot, muffled, but distinct in the dead-cold air, erupted from what sounded like the Bluebird Saloon.

"Whitaker!" someone shouted.

But Slocum was already on his way there, with one person in mind, and it wasn't Torrance Whitaker. "Hella," he whispered, thundering toward the Bluebird Saloon.

31

Moments before the crowd erupted in cheers, Hella rapped hard on Torrance Whitaker's office door at the back of the Bluebird Saloon.

"First one through that door I'll shoot, I swear it!"

Hella sneered at Torrance Whitaker's fat shout—even his voice sounded fat to her. "Whitaker, it's Hella Bridger. Let me in so I can explain this thing. You need to keep your head down just now, stay put, and let me help protect you. It's just a matter of time before that mob of drunken loggers makes its way over here and tries to pull you out the keyhole."

She heard no response. "I'm coming in." She hefted her own revolver in one hand, kept her rifle cradled in the crook of the other arm, and tried the knob. It turned and in she walked, hugging the door frame.

The office was dark, but she knew he was in there, heard his fat man breaths, quick and shallow. He even breathes fat, she thought. "Whitaker? Light a lamp, will you? We need to make plans to barricade this door, just in case

Slocum doesn't have any luck in making those lunkheaded loggers listen to him."

"Don't come any closer!"

The shout came straight from the back of the room. She heard a squawk—had to be his chair—and then there was a flash of fire and she felt a pain like she'd never felt before drive into her left shoulder, high up. It spun her half out the door frame, and she dropped the rifle and revolver.

It took Hella a few moments to come around to the full realization of the situation. "Whitaker," she said in a voice much softer than she meant it to sound. "You bastard—you shot me . . ." She felt cold, then warm all over, and a pulsing pain that kept growing worse. The stink of gun smoke hung heavy in the air.

Then he was standing over her. "Damn, you are a fat one," she said, then felt herself losing consciousness.

From the street, Whitaker heard shouts closing in, drawing closer to the Bluebird. "They're coming," he wheezed. "Oh no, what have I done? What do I do now?" He wrung his fat, sweaty hands together, then saw Hella's revolver. He grunted, snatched it off the floor, and saw her, still breathing. Good, just unconscious.

He grabbed the back of her collar, couldn't help noticing how pretty she was, even in the darkly lit, smoky office, and dragged her toward the back door. It led to the alley the businesses on that side of the street all used for deliveries. The alley itself backed right up to the near hill that the town was built up against.

Had to get out, use her somehow as a shield. Block them with her, keep them away from him until he could explain it all. That's the plan, he thought—have to get out of here, hole up. Maybe Jordan will have an idea. Have to get out of here, can't be caught inside.

He fought with the doorknob, realized it was locked, and fidgeted with the deadbolt. Finally it sprang open and he dragged the flopped woman on out into the snowy alley. It took a whole lot of doing, dragging that woman backward up the hill. He switchbacked, grunting and letting out low squeals, cursing the town, his son, McGee, everybody.

What was happening? Everything seemed to be falling apart, just like all the other towns. But this time it felt final, like he might not have another shot at money if he didn't make this work out somehow.

He heard the crowd thundering through his beloved Bluebird Saloon, figured he could make it over the top of the little hill, not once thinking that his tracks as well as those of the dragging feet of the trapper woman would be seen all the way up. He didn't care; he just had to get her away from there.

Maybe he could say he found her that way; maybe it was self-defense. Everyone knew she was a crazy, wild woman; maybe he could convince them that she had attacked him! Yes, that was just the story he'd use.

At the top of the hill he paused, flopped backward in the snow, the woman falling across his legs. He'd just wait here, let the crazy woman bleed. He didn't care a whit about her. He'd tell them all she attacked him and chased him up here, so he shot her. That was the plan, a good one. As good as he was likely to come up with anyway.

Whitaker closed his eyes as he lay in the snow, the bleeding woman still draped across his legs, and he worked to catch his breath before the crowd barreled through the Bluebird, past his office, out the back door, then on up the hill toward him.

A shadow fell across his face. He opened his eyes and looked up to see a face he'd never seen. And one he didn't believe was real. And then Torrance Whitaker realized in the flash of an instant that he would never have to worry about amassing a fortune ever again.

As the huge, freakish, hairy face descended on him, he screamed, screamed so loud for mere seconds that his throat shredded, began to blow out. And then the huge hairy thing lifted him high, high, high . . . and even though his voice had left him, Whitaker felt himself being ripped apart, limb from limb and limb from torso. And he kept on screaming, no sound coming from his bloody mouth. But he watched as his agony erupted in a spray of red against the high, blue mountain sky, as it colored the tops of the tall, tall trees at the very edge of his vision.

32

"I'll tell you just one more time, Hella. Then you have to get some rest." Slocum tucked the quilt up under her chin and set the cup of tea down beside her bed.

"By the time I got up there at the top of the hill just behind the buildings in Timber Hills, there you were, flopped in the snow, but breathing."

"Obviously," she said, rolling her eyes, but smirking, too.

"And," he continued, "there was a whole lot of blood everywhere, and not a few parts and pieces of what had once been Torrance Whitaker. And leading away from the mess, straight up into these hills . . ."

"Yes?" she said, like a little kid hearing the same ghost story every night.

"Tracks. Maybe a bear? Maybe . . . something clsc? What do you think?"

Hella smiled and closed her eyes, sinking back into her pillow. "I never said anything about skoocooms . . ."

Slocum stood quietly and went to the fireplace, stirred a bubbling pot of stew. It looked like he'd be stuck in this warm mountain cabin with this Crazy Trapper Lady for the rest of the winter. Once again, John Slocum shook his head, wondering how it was that he'd come to end up here, safe and sound in big timber country—surrounded by wild beasts of all sizes and shapes.

As if in response to his thoughts, from the woods all about the little cozy cabin a ragged chorus of growls and shrieks filled the chill night air.

Watch for

**SLOCUM AND THE WANTON WIDOWS
OF WOLF CREEK**

429th novel in the exciting SLOCUM series
from Jove

Coming in November!

DON'T MISS A YEAR OF

Slocum Giant
by
Jake Logan

penguin.com/actionwesterns

M457AS0812

LONGARM

GIANT-SIZED ADVENTURE FROM AVENGING ANGEL LONGARM.

BY TABOR EVANS

penguin.com/actionwesterns

M456AS0812

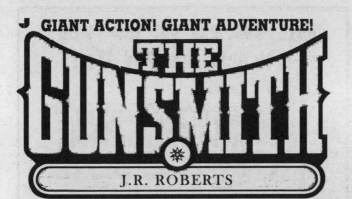

GIANT ACTION! GIANT ADVENTURE!

THE GUNSMITH

J.R. ROBERTS

penguin.com/actionwesterns

M455AS0812

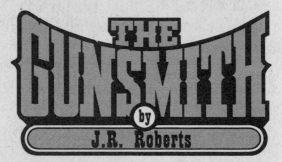